BY THE

BAY

EAST BEACH STORIES

BY THE BAY
East Beach Stories

Written by members of the
East Beach Writers Guild:

Gina Warren Buzby
Patrick Clark
Michelle Davenport
Karen Harris
Will Hopkins
R. G. Koepf
Mary-Jac O'Daniel
Jayne Ormerod
Mike Owens
Jenny F. Sparks

Foreword by Juanita Smith

Cover art Scene: East Beach Dunes
Medium: Oil on Canvas
By Gina Warren Buzby, Professional Artist
Permission licensed to Bay Breeze Publishing, LLC
for book cover and marketing materials
related to *By the Bay: East Beach Stories.*
All other rights reserved.

ISBN: ISBN-13: 978-0692466759
ISBN-10: 0692466754

Published by
Bay Breeze Publishing, LLC
Norfolk, VA
www.BayBreezePublishing.com

ABOUT THE BOOK

By the Bay, East Beach Stories is a collection of twelve fictional tales about life along the Chesapeake Bay. They range from murderous to romantic, from humorous to dramatic, from gritty noir to political thriller to the sweet and the spiritual. The thread that ties them together is their connection to a 100-acre peninsula in Norfolk, Virginia. East Beach is nestled on the shores of the southernmost point of the Chesapeake Bay, just as it becomes the Atlantic Ocean. Written by members of the East Beach Writers Guild, these tales exhibit the writers' love of their neighborhood and their talent for story-telling.

All proceeds from the sales of both electronic and trade paperback versions of this books will be disbursed to reading-related non-profits in the Norfolk, Virginia area. For information on disbursements, please visit our blog: www.BytheBayStories.blogspot.com.

ACKNOWLEDGEMENTS

"There are two kinds of editors,
Those who correct your copy,
And those who say, "It's wonderful."

~Theodore White

The members of the East Beach Writers' Guild would like to thank independent editors James M. Warren, CB Lane and Elizabeth Kimball for being both critical and encouraging. Their expert eyes and honest feedback made all of our stories stronger.

TABLE OF CONTENTS

FOREWORD

BY JUANITA SMITH

"What kind of community is this?" asked my friend, Mary, as I turned onto Pleasant Avenue, the main street that runs parallel to the bay and through the center of the East Beach community where I live.

"What kind of question is that?" I asked.

"Is this a new neighborhood made to look old or an old neighborhood made to look new?" she asked as we came to the end of the windshield tour of my neighborhood.

"It's a new neighborhood with the traditional architectural design of Tidewater homes in the early 1900s. It's called New Urbanism," I replied, silently chuckling at her question.

"Each house is different yet similar. It looks like a magazine picture or a movie set. Everything is picture perfect. Almost too pretty to be real," Mary mused, giving her own summation about the neighborhood. "What kinds of people live here? The houses are so close together with the front porches almost encroaching onto the narrow streets," Mary thoughtfully observed.

"All kinds," I replied.

"It's a great mix, everyone from judges, state and local elected officials, to military families and retirees, everyday people and everyone in-between. The community was intentionally designed to appeal to a wide variety of owners so there is a style of house to fit almost anyone. Owners have one thing in common here: they want to live a simple life on the Chesapeake Bay. Like the architecture, each neighbor is different yet similar, but all with unique and interesting stories to tell," I said.

"Do neighbors really sit on their porches and talk to one another like in the olden days?" she asked.

"Yeah, we really do. Not only do we talk to our next-door neighbors, we talk to friends walking along the street pushing strollers or riding in their golf carts full of beach paraphernalia on their way to the beach. I know many of my neighbors by name and their dogs' names too. It seems most families have a dog and some have two," I said. "East Beach etiquette dictates that when introducing yourself to a new neighbor, you first introduce yourself to the neighbor; then after saying your name you introduce your dog. That took a little getting used to for me."

That bit of dry humor was lost on Mary. That whole idea escaped her as she continued to mentally dissect the community. My "perfect community" was hard for her to wrap her mind around.

East Beach is not only a home to those who share

the common desire to live a simple life on the Chesapeake Bay; but it is also a community of writers. Many are published authors who have written for a variety of media. Others are timid beginners in search of their voices, but still they write.

By the Bay is an anthology of short stories written by members of the East Beach Writers Guild. The anthology fits in the general category of Beach Books–the kind of easy-to-read books taken to the beach or poolside. Each story has enough plot to hold the reader's attention but is light enough to induce relaxation in the sun. This non-traditional anthology has a twist to it. While most beach books are about adventures of people who go to the beach, the stories in this book are written from the perspective of those who may not have been born there but who now live at the beach and write stories about life "by the bay."

The story of East Beach itself and its residents is intriguing. East Beach is located on a 100-acre peninsula in the Ocean View section of Norfolk. At least two decades ago, local city officials and developers realized that this was prime waterfront property wasting away as a result of decades of neglect, overbuilding and crime. After years of strategizing, the city and the developers put plans in place to clear the land and create a new community designed like an old-fashioned coastal village. The plan created a vibrant, interactive community that brought back a simple lifestyle on the Chesapeake Bay.

This New Urbanism master plan quickly attracted the attention of a diverse group of people from many points along the East Coast and beyond. People of every walk of life were captivated by East Beach, partly because of the imagination and creativity that went into its design.

Once the community was established, it wasn't long before a common thread was identifiable among the new owners: many had a story to tell and wanted to share those stories in writing. The idea to publish a collection of fictional stories set in East Beach was not a hard sell.

Surprisingly, without the knowledge of one another, six of the ten authors wrote murder mysteries! Who would have thought that writers living in perfectly designed Chesapeake Bay homes with pastel painted front doors and shutters would be tucked away inside, hunched over their computers, intently imagining murder mystery plots?

One example is "Boneyard" by Patrick Clark. This is a story about a landscaper, who, while digging a hole to plant a large tree in the backyard of a new residence, finds a long-ago buried human skull. For those of us who live here and are familiar with seemingly on-going landscaping projects, the story is particularly intriguing.

Given the roles canines play in this neighborhood, the anthology would be incomplete without a dog story—told from the dog's perspective, of course. Jenny Sparks pens a story titled "Millie's Missing Key." It's about how a dog and her person's ordinary day is upended when the person can't find her house key. The hunt for the key sets the stage for the neighborhood dogs to talk, socialize and flirt a bit.

The members of the East Beach Writers Guild are great storytellers. The stories are sometimes so realistic that one wonders if they could possibly have some element of truth. Well, you decide.

This collection of short stories introduces the reader to an unusual, but "perfect" community by the Chesapeake Bay. One with an eclectic group of resident writers who write stories that are entertaining and stimulating, while also giving the reader a picture of life not just on the Chesapeake Bay but also from the very special, "perfect" East Beach perspective. This is a wonderful book to stick in your bag and head to the beach or poolside, settling in for a few hours of relaxation and fun reading. I hope reading the stories in **By the Bay** will raise your curiosity about this "perfect" community and the people who live here. Who knows, one day I might greet you from my perfect front porch as you stroll past my house, coming to just check out the neighborhood.

~Juanita Smith

JUANITA SMITH is a retired Executive Director of Human Resources for the Defense Logistics Agency; President of Kingdom Building Equipping School, a former teacher of the East Beach Bible study group and author of the book, What I Believe.

Juanita has a unique connection to what is now called East Beach. More than 60 years ago, as a child, she played on this beach at a time when it was then called City Beach. Her grandparents were beach caretakers who lived in a cinderblock house behind the chain-link fence that enclosed the beach. Their job was to open the gate in the morning and close it in the evening after the last beach-goers left. An annual visit to her grandparents' house was considered her "summer vacation". Juanita, her siblings, and cousins, spent many happy days playing on the hot sand, splashing in the shallow waters of the Chesapeake Bay, crabbing and climbing the large rocks that separated the bay from the Little Creek Channel where navy ships and commercial boats crisscross daily.

She is a Norfolk native, who, after graduating from Norfolk State University and working locally for twenty-five years as a civil servant for the Navy in Human Resources, moved to Alexandria, Virginia, where she was promoted to a Senior Executive Service position for the Department of Defense. After retirement, Juanita and her husband, Willie, decided to relocate to Norfolk, with the thought of purchasing a condo by the bay.

Their search for a beachfront condo did not go as they planned. They consider it serendipitous that they discovered a community called East Beach, still in the development stage. A builder friend showed them blueprints of a large brick house situated on an unpaved street close to the bay. Though it was not quite what they initially imagined for a retirement home, it felt right and it was clearly a wonderful opportunity. In a matter of days, they contracted to purchase it and became the first East Beach homeowners.

It was only after the purchase of their "house by the bay" did Juanita experience an epiphany. She suddenly realized: "This is the old City Beach, the place where my grandparents lived in the '50s and where I, as a child, spent my summers playing on the hot sand." The small cinderblock house they lived in had been replaced by a construction staging area, but the locked chain-link fence, and more importantly, the memories were still firmly in place. She had come a long way from summers spent with family on City Beach to retirement at East Beach.

She says, "Finding East Beach was like going to the beach looking for a particular grain of sand—and finding it."

PLEIN MYSTERIOUS

By Gina Warren Buzby

I was sweating bullets because I needed to finish my painting of the bay before the looming Plein Air Festival deadline. Little did I know that before day's end I would see *real* bullets *and* bullet holes!

Painting *en plein air* (French for "in the open air," pronounced "on plain air" in English) means you have a unique set of challenges as an artist painting outdoors. You have to fight the wind, heat or cold, the moving light, the mosquitoes, and the clock. So, it's important to set up your easel early in the day, along with paints, palette, brushes, and accessories in order to have ample time to overcome these variables and finish a good painting. Oh, and did I mention the deadline? It was time for the annual Norfolk Plein Air Festival, and the deadline was the next day. Lots of artists were out and about in different locations around Norfolk, trying to finish a maximum of three paintings in two and a half days. I was going to be happy with just finishing one.

In the late 1800s, the Impressionists made *en plein air*

1

painting a popular choice for art admirers and collectors. It has since evolved into a specific genre of the painting world. An *en plein air* painting indicates that the artist has worked directly from outdoor life with none of today's digital enhancements or assistance. I did take some photographs during the week before the competition so that I would have the correct composition and light recorded. This was insurance in case weather or a schedule change prevented me from returning in time. This particular festival did allow for at least 25% of the painting to be finished in the studio. But, I'm a purist, so I was back in that same exact spot where I'd begun the painting. Besides, I prefer painting *en plein air*, especially at East Beach. The beach runs from east to west, allowing for some spectacular sunrises and sunsets.

In preparation, I wore bug spray, sunscreen, my favorite "It's Ok, I'm An Artist" T-shirt, cargo shorts, and flip-flops. It seemed that I had beaten most everyone out to the beach, except for a few power walkers heading west away from the hot, rising sun. Thankfully, my boss at the gallery was covering for me and my apartment rental was just a few steps from the beach. My easy, early start was proving to be just what I needed to finish the painting, allow for drying time, framing, and turning it into the festival coordinators before the deadline. And hopefully, sell it for a nice price that would help with rent this month.

As the sunrise haze lifted, the humidity and heat quickly had me "glistening" (as my southern mother prefers to say) in my ball cap, ponytail and no make-up. But, I was excited about the dramatic lighting I would soon recreate on my canvas.

As I pulled on my splotchy, paint-covered apron and sat in my chair, I looked out at the landscape in order to relocate my started painting's perspective. The morning hues inspired me, so I picked up my brushes while noting the most important shades to add to my canvas. Color and light fascinate me, as I think they do most artists. I notice them everywhere. I began mixing colors on my palette. I appreciated the golden (raw sienna) light of the rising sun coming through the oak trees on the opposite side of the channel. A part of the Naval Amphibious Base Little Creek was directly across the creek and stood out with its high concrete walls. Instead, I focused on the trees at the wall's edge and the point where the hovercraft launches were visible. The point was bordered by sea oats and grasses with their sunlit pink and amber glow that I would include.

And, I'd leave out that ugly, concrete (charcoal grey) wall. Artistic license!

It was lovely. The sunlight glittered diamond-like (cadmium yellow) on the small, sapphire (Prussian blue) currents of the waterway. The violet (purple lake) shadows cast by the trees and bushes onto the beach were dramatic and a must to include. Then, there was that shock of pink (magenta) floating on top of the creek. As I strained to see over the breakwater, I realized that shock of pink was a scarf. A lady's floral scarf. And there looked to be a woman floating, face down, attached to said scarf! The current was carrying her slowly down the side of the rocky breakwater.

I dropped my palette and ran over to stand on the

rocks where I could see the body better. I had to be sure my eyes weren't deceiving me. Sure enough, it definitely was a body, face down, lifeless, in the water. She looked to be wearing a lavender pantsuit.

I screamed for help. No one heard me; the power walkers were gone. There were some fishermen on a boat way down the creek, but they couldn't hear me.

I awkwardly hopped off the rocks, ran back to the easel, grabbed my cell phone and shakily dialed 9-1-1.

"Th—th—there's a body floating in Little Creek!" I stuttered.

"Are you sure it's a body?" asked the emergency call center operator.

No, it's a sea turtle dressed in lavender (cobalt violet)!

"Let's put it this way, it looks like a floating woman, fully-dressed, unmoving and face down in the water! And, I can't get close enough because of the jagged breakwater, but it is floating toward the Bay Point private docks!"

Ok, so truth be told, I am a bit prissy. Sure, I will get paint on me and mess around with turpentine, etc. But, generally, I like things tidy, neat, anti-bacterial—and alive, not dead. So, to say I should have reached out and pulled in that body would be hilarious to me. No thanks. I was shaking as it was. Plus, I am sure my small frame couldn't have lifted that much bigger, floating woman. And, I wouldn't have wanted to hinder the investigation with my messy fingerprints, don't you know.

As some of the nearby residents began running over, one of them carried a first-aid kit. *It's not going to help in this situation, but it is a nice effort.* Two anxious fishermen came running over from a nearby dock. They had heard me scream and point. Those two fellas were ready to get a rope and "pull 'em in!" More power to them.

At that moment, the ambulance and police cars started to pull up to the beach. None of the bystanders had touched the body yet (I felt justified), they were just pointing at the dead woman and then over toward me. I knew someone would need to question me but I really didn't want to see how this was going to turn out. Remember, I'm *prissy*. I don't like watching *CSI*, *SVU*, *Breaking Bad* and all that bloody, dead-body stuff on TV. They give me nightmares.

I was fairly new to the neighborhood, so I was sure it was no one I knew. I had also quickly figured out that my painting efforts had been thwarted. So I, sadly, ambled over to my easel and started packing up my *plein air* equipment.

As I replaced the oil paints back into their drawer, a tall, dark, and handsome man walked my way. What can I say? It's the only way to describe him. He was at least six feet tall with wavy dark brown (burnt sienna) hair that bounced a little when he walked.

He presented his badge to me in a John Wayne kind of way. And, in a low, Barry White voice he said, "Hi, I am Detective Addison."

"Hi," I said. "I'm Lizzy Warren."

I was still shaking but already thinking if we had a little boy I could use my maiden name as a first name (southerners do that a lot) and he'd be Warren Addison— oooh, I liked that! But, I quickly came back to reality as Detective Addison handed me his business card.

His first name is William…hmmm, is he Will?

He asked, "You called nine-one-one, right, Mrs. Warren?"

"Oh, I did, but, it's *Miss* Warren." I couldn't help but smile.

"Do you mind telling me the events of this morning?"

"I am actually feeling a little light-headed. It's probably the heat. Do you mind if we sit down somewhere?" I asked.

"Would you prefer an EMT look you over first?"

"No, thanks. I'll be fine, I just don't find dead people floating in my painting compositions every day."

"There's some shade under the stairs of that public walkover. I'll have some chairs brought over. Let's go sit there and I'll also have someone bring you a bottle of water," he said.

The shade did look inviting as I realized I was a little dizzy from the heat and the drama. I gladly let him support me by holding my elbow—*E-lec-tricity*—as we walked to the shade. I felt lightheaded and yet euphoric. Two beach chairs appeared and were placed under the wood-planked stairs. This cool, blue (French ultramarine) spot is where *we* would sit *together* and get to know each other. Yes, that's right, there was a dead body in the creek right in front of us. But romance is everywhere, especially when you're single and over thirty-five. A uniformed police officer came over with a chilled bottle of water. I thanked him and he left.

The cold water was a godsend. I explained to Detective Addison—*William*—that I had just arrived, set up my easel and noticed the scarf in the water. As I recounted my morning walk to the beach and set-up routine, I noticed the emergency medical team pulling out the body while the police were taking photos and taping off the dunes and a section of the breakwater. Some of the earlier power walkers had been tracked down and corralled into a group next to an old, beached catamaran. They were being questioned by two other detectives. My detective was the cutest. Oh, and those green (viridian) eyes! *Why, oh why, hadn't I put on some make-up?* Although, in that heat, it wouldn't have mattered.

William—yes, we were on a first-name basis already thanks to my persistence—wrote down all of the information he needed and escorted me past the crime scene. While he was making notes, I noticed a very big gun in a holster, extra bullets on a belt attachment, very nice hand-writing, but most importantly, no wedding ring! I tore my mind from future wedding plans and glanced over at the guys carrying the body board dripping with bay water and holding the retrieved, wet, dead body.

It wasn't a woman I had seen floating in the creek after all. It was a man. I could see his chiseled features, albeit a little bluish, with a small goatee and a head full of black (Payne's grey) hair. The pink floral scarf, wrapped around his neck, was a Gucci. Or at least a knock-off. I wish I could tell the fake designer stuff from the real. I can't afford either.

"Mr. Dead" looked to be a flashy dresser. His suit was lavender (pale mauve) and his shoes were once white but now covered in mud. His lips were oddly swollen and a weird shade of violet. His skin was a pale blue (cerulean) and almost matched his suit in places, except for the black bullet hole on his forehead. My, how my color references had changed from earlier that day. I needed to get out of here. I was already going to have to take several Tylenol PMs in order to sleep tonight.

Later, after a Michelob Light under the air-conditioning and then a hot shower, I reflected on the day.

The *good* news was that I had exchanged phone numbers with a nice, gainfully employed, handsome, single man. And he had already called me. Yes, twice! Once to tell me "Mr. Dead" was a missing drug dealer from across the bay. The dealer must have made an enemy or two along the way because the scarf had been used to strangle him before he'd ended up in the indigo blue water.

The second call was to ask me to dinner.

The *bad* news was I left the beach minus a finished painting, and with lots of *CSI* fodder for new nightmares.

BONEYARD

By Patrick Clark

JULY 2014

Perfect. Everything is just perfect.

Heather Kroft was making her final walkthrough with the builder of her newly constructed bay-front home in the East Beach neighborhood of Norfolk, Virginia. She stood in the kitchen and inspected the details to ensure that all of her specifications had been met. The natural white oak hardwood floors complemented the plum colored walls, dark cherry cabinets and beige granite countertops. *Check.* The large panoramic window that faced the Chesapeake Bay provided plenty of natural light and offered spectacular views of the water. *Check.*

This was her dream house. She and her husband, Tom, had worked hard to get to this point. Heather was a successful dentist and worked in a local partnership. Tom was a financial analyst who had weathered the recession and the bear market, and now that the market had rebounded, was easily bringing in a six-figure income. Both in their mid-thirties, they'd agreed it was time to start a family, and this was the house and the neighborhood where they wanted to do that.

Tom was in the great room going over the details of the closing process with the builder. Heather could hear them talking but was not paying any attention to what they were saying. It was just background noise for the moment.

Outside, the landscaping crew was planting a row of feather reed grass with a dwarf magnolia tree at each end, directly in front of the beach dune. This would serve to identify the property line as well as stem the encroachment of beach sand into the Kroft's small backyard.

Heather leaned back on the kitchen island that faced the panoramic view and surveyed the scene. She admired the shirtless, muscular young man on the landscaping crew. *So what if you just read* Fifty Shades of Grey, *you can't think like that!*

She pulled back her blonde hair and placed a band around her ponytail, then rested her chin in her cupped hand, her smile hidden behind her fingers bent at the knuckle under her nose. She felt her blue eyes moisten, just a little.

Yes. Everything is perfect.

The planting hole for the dwarf magnolia needed to be 18 inches wide and 24 inches deep. The landscaping crew chief had assigned the task to Carl Malone. Carl was a rising senior at Old Dominion University and he loved this summer job. He particularly enjoyed being outdoors and working his muscles while drawing a nice paycheck for seasonal work.

Carl prepared the planting hole by starting with an 18 inch wide circle and then digging down to the required depth. He stood inside the circle with his foot on the top of the shovel blade, wiped the sweat off of his forehead with the back of his arm, and inhaled deeply. The earthy smell of the freshly churned soil mixed with the fresh breeze of the bay.

A few more shovels full should do it.

He pushed his foot heavily on the shovel.

Clink. The blade of the shovel impacted something metallic, and after the dirt shifted and settled, Carl noticed a gold colored object had been partially unearthed.

"What the hell is that?" He bent closer to look at it. He swiped his finger along the object a few times, which exposed it a little more, and determined the object was flat with some kind of scene depicted on the surface. He swiped away some more of the sand and soil mixture and was able to get his hands under the object and pull it free from the ground. As he wiped off the remaining dirt he discovered a heavy brass plate, about one-quarter-inch thick and nine inches in diameter. An engraving on the flat surface depicted a crab, what looked like WWII mines, and the name USS Guide.

Interesting. This thing must weigh at least ten pounds.

Carl set the plate aside and again pushed his foot heavily on the shovel and then used his leg strength to lift the shovel and deposit the fresh soil in a small pile outside of the planting hole. The soil around the newly evacuated area shifted, and some fell off the sides, exposing what appeared to be the facial side of a human skull.

"What the Helsinki?" he uttered.

Is that what I think it is?

He got on his knees and used his hands to partially clear the area around the skull and confirmed the object was what he thought it was.

"Damn! This can't be good."

Carl stood and shouted toward his crew chief, "Rory, you need to get over here! We have a problem!"

Rory Calhoun was a big guy. He was about six-feet three-inches tall, barrel chested, and had wide shoulders and large biceps. Rory liked his beer and had a waistline consistent with a fifty-year-old man who had spent his life doing outdoor manual labor during the day and kicking back with his brew in the evening.

Rory stood shirtless on the backyard deck with a view of the beach and was admiring a trio of young bikini-clad girls strolling at the water's edge on the beach.

"This better be important, Malone. I'm enjoying the view of things from here."

One of the girls leaned over and splashed the other two, which resulted in screaming and giggling laughter.

"Rory, I mean it, man. This is a no-shit problem, dude. You need to get over here!"

"Aw, shit." *Goddamn college kids can't figure out how to plant a damn tree?*

Rory took one last look at the girls, rolled his eyes, and marched across the deck, down the steps, across the yard and stood next to the planting hole, towering over Carl, who was still standing in the hole.

"So what's the goddamn crisis?"

Carl looked up at Rory and stepped out of the way. He said nothing as he rubbed the back of his neck with his dirty left hand and pointed at the skull with his right.

"I'll be damned! Is that a human head?"

"Sure's hell looks like one to me," replied Carl.

"Shit! I've been diggin' holes damn near my whole life and I ain't ever had this happen before. You need to get out of there, kid. We probably need to rope this off and call the cops."

Carl sat on the edge of the hole with his legs over the side and pushed himself to a standing position.

Rory hollered to a third person on the work crew. "Manny! Stop what you're doing and go back to the truck. Bring me about half a dozen planter sticks. Four foot long. And some rope."

"I found this brass plate, too." Carl pointed to the plate lying where he had tossed it next to the dirt pile. "You think we should sift through the dirt and see if there's anything else in there?"

"Nah. Don't do that. Let's leave that for the cops."

Manuel "Manny" Rodriguez arrived with the sticks and rope. "So what's goin' on, boss?"

"See for yourself," said Rory as he pointed toward the exposed skull.

Manny leaned his head forward as if the extra inches would provide a better view. "Shit! That's a skull!"

"Thank you for that, Captain Obvious," replied Rory. "You guys stake this out and rope it off. I think I saw the owners with the builder's lead, Bob Hewlett. I'll go tell 'em. Ain't nobody gonna be happy about this."

From her seat at the kitchen island, Heather watched the landscapers' unusual activity. She noted with some trepidation that the well-built young guy had stopped digging and held an animated discussion with the team lead. Now the whole crew was roping off the area. Although she was not an expert in planting trees, something about this didn't look right. When she noticed the team lead had put his shirt back on and was now marching toward the back door of the house, she pushed herself off her perch on the island counter and walked toward the great room.

"Tom, I think there may be a problem with the landscaping. Someone is coming to the back door. I think he wants to talk to you."

Rory reached the back door and lifted his knuckles to rap on the glass just as Tom Kroft and Bob Hewlett opened the door from inside.

"Afternoon, Mr. Hewlett."

"Afternoon, Rory. Have you met Mr. Kroft? He's the new homeowner."

Heather ambled up behind them.

"And Mrs. Kroft," Tom added.

"Afternoon, sir, ma'am. It's a beautiful home."

"Thank you," replied Tom.

"Mr. Hewlett, may I have a word with you please? Out by the landscaping?"

"Is there a problem, Rory?"

"Be best if I show you."

Hewlett frowned slightly "Sure. Lead the way."

Rory and Bob Hewlett, with Tom close behind, walked toward the planting hole.

"Bob, I hate to break this to ya, but we found something that will probably delay the landscape phase by a bit. And, I think we'll also probably need to call the police."

"What?" Hewlett's eyes narrowed and he tilted his head slightly.

The trio reached the planting hole and Rory pointed toward the exposed skull. "Well, see for yourself. I think we've dug up a human skeleton. At least as much as a skull."

"Son of a bi—," uttered Hewlett as he peered over the side of the hole toward the skull. "Never had this happen before. I don't know what the protocol is for this kind of thing, but yeah, I'm sure it starts with a call to the police."

Kroft stood, his lips pursed and his arms folded across his chest. "How much of a delay?" he asked.

TWO DAYS LATER

"Cole, why don't you put your desk so you can face the window?" suggested Katie Draper, the irreverent niece of the recently retired FBI Special Agent who was setting up his new private investigation office. "Only a monk would put their back to the window, and you are not a monk."

"Because, Katie dear, when I'm working, I will have the blinds closed. When I am not working, I will not be in this office to enjoy the wonderful view of Pretty Lake Avenue."

"Well, why don't you—" she started to say before Cole cut her off.

"Why don't you hang those pictures where I asked you to?"

"Do I get to choose the pictures that will hang in my area?"

"We've been through this, Katie, you are not going to be my assistant. You're going to finish college and go on to be the world's greatest marine biologist."

They both turned toward the slight knocking at the outer door.

"I'll get it," said Katie as she hurried out of the back office where they had been setting up, through the small receptionist area that was not yet complete, and to the outer door.

Katie pulled the rubber band out of her long black ponytail and let her hair fall down over her shoulders. *This looks a little more professional,* she thought. After taking a moment to adjust her V-neck Old Dominion University T-shirt to ensure that only a professional amount of cleavage was showing, Katie opened the door inward.

"Can I help you?"

"Yes. I'm looking for a Mr. Cole Draper. Is this his office?"

"Yes, ma'am. I'm Katie, Mr. Draper's assistant. I'll see if he is available."

"Nice try, Katie," said Cole as he walked up behind her. "I'm Cole Draper," he said as he slipped past Katie and extended his hand to the visitor. "And you are?"

"My name is Heather Kroft." She extended her hand to complete the handshake. "I saw on the East Beach community website that a private investigation firm had just opened. Then I saw your name on the door yesterday as I walked past. I have a matter that I'd like to see if you could help me with."

"I'll certainly try. Please come into my office and we'll talk about it." Cole led her through the reception area. "As you can see, Ms. Kroft, I'm still getting things set up. I actually just took possession a few days ago."

As they walked together, Cole did an initial assessment of Ms. Heather Kroft, just as he had done on hundreds of victims and criminals in his twenty years with the FBI. Heather Kroft was a very attractive woman. Her blond shoulder-length hair, blue eyes, and high cheekbones were almost doll perfect. She was poised, and held her back and shoulders straight as she walked. The tight jeans and high heels accentuated her shapely behind and the red silk shirt hung loosely over her toned shoulders. She had all of the characteristics of a well-bred and well-educated woman. The carats she wore on her left ring finger left no doubt about her financial bracket or her availability for a romantic dinner.

"Katie, can you get me a bottle of water? Ms. Kroft, can I get you something to drink?" asked Cole.

"A bottle of water would be nice. Thank you."

"Katie, two bottles, please."

"Is that something an assistant would do?" asked Katie.

Cole responded with a deadly serious, stern look.

"Okay! Two bottles of water. Jeeesh."

Cole pulled a recently delivered rose-colored armchair out of the corner of the room, tore off the plastic covering and tossed that aside near the wastebasket. "Ms. Kroft, please sit here," he said as he moved the chair forward for her.

Cole noticed her smile and heard a small giggle.

"Please, call me Heather." Her smile broadened. "You really are just getting set up, aren't you?"

Katie returned and handed each of them a bottle of water. "Two bottles of water, boss." She quickly departed.

Cole pulled his brown leather executive chair around the desk to face Heather and asked, "What can I do for you?"

"Well, Mr. Draper."

"Please call me Cole."

"Very well then, Cole. My husband and I purchased a beachfront home here in East Beach. It's the yellow one with white trim a few houses away from the Ship's Cabin restaurant."

"I've seen it. Congratulations. It looks like a beautiful house."

"Thanks. It is, but there is one big problem. At least

it is for me." She took a drink from her water bottle and Cole leaned forward toward her. "A few days ago, the landscapers unearthed human remains."

Cole sat back in his chair, his arms on the armrests. "Ah-huh. I heard about that. I had dinner at A.J. Gators last night. People were talking about it. Everyone seemed to have a harebrained speculation about who it was and what the circumstances were. What have the police said?"

Heather looked toward the floor and began to rub her temples with her fingertips. "I'm probably overreacting but this has me really disturbed. Haven't slept much since this happened."

"Understandable," Cole replied. "Have you spoken to the police?"

"Yes. Detective Hartman is the lead on this."

"Les Hartman. I know him. He's a good detective."

Heather looked up, and Cole made eye contact with her before she spoke. "He said it looked like it was going to be assigned to the Cold Case department. He told me the remains appeared to be an adult male and that forensics would try to match the remains with a missing person's case. But, Detective Hartman also advised me that the remains looked like they had been there for a long time. He told me not to get my hopes up about a quick resolution."

"The police will do everything they can to resolve this."

"I know. But that may take some time. Like I said, I'm probably overreacting. My husband certainly thinks so, Mr. Draper—"

"Please call me Cole."

"Yes." She paused a moment, her mouth tight as she bit her lip. "Cole. I won't feel comfortable living there until I know who this person was and what happened to him. Can you look into this and give it a higher priority than the police will?"

Cole clasped his fingers behind his head and breathed out. There was a long silence while he thought about his answer. He then leaned forward, picked up his water bottle from the desk and took a long drink, twisted the cap back on and then set it down. "Heather, I should be honest with you. My target clientele is large corporations or government entities, so if there is a criminal case here, it would be handled best by the police. I'm sure that you understand if this is a cold case, several if not many years have passed, so there is no immediate danger for you and your family to live there."

"I know that, Cole. I just need closure. I keep thinking about it. What if he had a family? Wouldn't they like to know?"

Cole remained silent for a few moments, considering his answer. Eventually he reached the conclusion. *Why not? I've got nothing else pressing right now.*

"Okay. I'll start tomorrow by talking to Detective Hartman."

"Thank you, Cole," replied Heather. "I'm very grateful. Do I need to write you a check or something?" she asked.

"No. Not yet. Let me talk with Hartman tomorrow. If I think I can help you, then I'll give you an estimate."

"That's fine. Thank you again, Cole." She handed him her business card. "Will you call me tomorrow?"

"Yes. Of course."

Heather stood and extended her hand for Cole to shake and she handed him her empty water bottle, which he tossed in the trash can.

"I can see myself out, Cole. Thank you again."

Cole watched her as she walked out the door. *That is one exceptionally attractive lady.*

"Do we have our first client?" asked Katie as she bolted through the door.

"Katie!"

The next morning, Cole sat at his small cherry wood desk in a small home office next to his bedroom and used his iPhone to call police headquarters.

A very pleasant female voice answered the phone. "Norfolk Police Investigative Services. How can I direct your call?"

"Hi, Jan, this is Cole Draper. You sound sexier than usual today."

"Cole…while it's always fun to hear from you, someday you're going to get one, or maybe both if us, in trouble," replied the division receptionist. "How's retirement treating you?"

"Can't complain. Golf game's getting better."

"That's great. Can't imagine that golf is all you've been up to, though."

"As a matter of fact, I did get my PI license and I've opened an office. With any luck, I'll get busy enough to have reason to visit you all quite often. Which, in fact, as much as I enjoy talking with you, is why I called. I'm working on a case and I need to talk to Les Hartman."

"Okay. I'll forward your call. Nice talking to you, Cole."

Cole listened to three buzzes before Hartman picked up. "Homicide, this is Hartman."

"Les. Cole Draper here. How's your day goin'?"

"Usual hot summer bullshit. Gangbangers with guns still providing me job security. So what happened to you? That was a pretty hasty retirement."

"It's a long story. Tell you over a beer someday."

"Okay. Whatever. So what's the purpose of this call?"

"Always to the point. Well, I've opened a private investigation firm, and I may take a case that I think you're the lead detective on, unless you've already handed it to cold cases."

"You talking about the skeleton found in East Beach?"

"That's the one."

"Yeah, well, interesting case. The kid who found the remains also found a heavy brass plate with a ship's name and hull number on it."

"A brass plate?" asked Cole.

"Yeah. Ya know, years ago, the ships' engineers used to take all of their scrap brass to a foundry and melt it down and cast these brass plates. They would then attach it to a plaque and give it to sailors on special occasions."

"Sounds pretty costly."

"Exactly. They stopped doing that. Now it's a plastic plaque. Anyway, from the way the skull was cracked in the back, I've got a pretty good feeling that someone used that brass plate to give the vic a damn good headache."

"Huh. Well that's interesting. So you believe it was a homicide?"

"Looks that way. So, because of the plate, I figured there must be some connection to the Navy, and I called Mark Garrison over at NCIS to see if he could make a connection. Garrison called back a few hours later and told me he might have something. Back in '78, a Petty Officer who had been assigned to the USS Guide, that's the ships name on the brass plate, went missing after he transferred from the ship. Let's see." Cole heard the sound of papers rustling. "The kid's name was Roger McLaren. Twenty-three years old. Enlisted in '73. His records show that the kid transferred from the Guide but never reported to his next assignment, which was supposed to be in South Carolina. The file said the last time he was seen was at his farewell party, which was probably when he was presented with this plaque. It also said he got pretty drunk at that party. Also, the kid was given a ten-thousand dollar reenlistment bonus and was never heard from again. The Navy figured he took the money and ran, so they declared him a deserter."

"So you think this may be him?" asked Cole.

"It's a pretty good lead. Forensics is trying to determine a match. Don't have any DNA to work with so they're going to have to match dental records. Military folks have always been pretty good at that. If this is McLaren, we should have a positive ID by tomorrow morning."

"Thanks, Les. You've been a big help."

"Hey, that's not all. In fact, it gets even more interesting."

"Oh?"

"I checked our cold cases for East Ocean View. There's a file from the same time frame that matches the Navy's case on McLaren. Our file said he apparently had a girlfriend, nineteen years old, according to a statement from one of her co-workers. She lived with McLaren, along with her sixteen-year-old sister. They also went missing. The case summary stated the most likely occurrence was that McLaren took off, and the girls went with him."

Cole rocked back in his swivel chair and ran his unencumbered hand through his hair. "So, are you going to reopen the case?"

"Don't know yet. Let's see if we get a positive ID. Call me again tomorrow and I'll bring you up to date. But, Cole…"

"Yeah?"

"Hope your new neighbor friend won't mind seeing a few more holes dug up in her yard."

"Thanks again, Les."

"Glad to help. Hey, Cole, if the PI thing don't work out, think about joining the force. I think you'd be a good detective."

Cole smiled and politely chuckled. "Thanks, Les. I'll keep that in mind. See ya."

The next day, Cole went for a long morning run

followed by an hour of moderate-intensity weight lifting in the East Beach fitness room. By 10:00 a.m., he had shaved, showered, and dressed in a conservative gray suit with a white shirt and red tie. He was a handsome man. Forty-three-years old, a solid six-feet one-inch, 220 pounds, he had deep brown eyes, light brown hair with a little grey coming in around the ears, worn short but not too short. Fit, with broad shoulders and a slim waist, he looked like he could still play tight end for his University of Virginia alma mater.

Cole decided that a personal visit and some face time with Hartman would be more productive than a phone call. *Maybe have lunch with him*, he thought as he finished his first cup of coffee while sitting on the balcony of his Each Beast Villa overlooking the Little Creek Harbor.

After a brief and mischievous phone conversation with Jan, the receptionist, he was patched through to Detective Hartman.

Since Hartman needed to visit the crime scene anyway, they decided to meet at the East Beach Sandwich Company for lunch and discuss updates to the case.

Cole was already seated at a high-top table in the outside eating area when Hartman arrived. After a brief handshake they each went to the counter, ordered sandwiches and returned to the high-top.

Hartman leaned his elbows on the table with his chin rested in his hand. "NCIS confirmed the dental records. The victim is this McLaren kid."

"Well, not unexpected," replied Cole. "So what are you gonna do now?"

"Start a crime scene excavation of the beach area near where McLaren was found."

"You think you'll find the girls, too?" asked Cole as he wiped a small bit of mayo from the corner of his mouth.

"I don't think so," Hartman answered with a whimsical smile. "But I do hope we can unearth some more clues about what happened and why."

Cole sensed there was something that Hartman wasn't saying. "What are you not telling me?"

"I have a name," answered Hartman, as he turned his head to the side and spoke out of the side of his mouth. "If you want to look into this, unofficially, I would start here. The girlfriend."

"Did the girlfriend have a name?"

"Yea…Paula Dorn."

Cole coughed a small amount of his chicken sandwich into a napkin. "You mean, two-time Grammy winner Paula Dorn?"

"It appears so. The deposition that I mentioned yesterday, from our file in '78, was from the headwaiter at the Ship's Cabin restaurant. That's where Paula Dorn worked when she was living with McLaren. We contacted him this morning and he confirmed that they are one and the same. In fact, he was very proud that he had once worked with such a talented singer. Said she was always singing while she was at work. Of course, he hadn't had any contact with her since then."

"You think she was involved in McLaren's murder?"

"It's a possibility," replied Hartman as he placed the uneaten remnants of his sandwich in a plastic tray. "She disappeared after McLaren was assumed to have deserted. Off the grid. Looks suspicious."

"Are you going to charge her?"

"With what? I don't have a case...yet."

Cole smiled because he now understood what Hartman was hoping to do. "So if someone were to visit Ms. Dorn and ask a few questions about her relationship with Petty Officer McLaren, she may possibly slip up and say or do something that could incriminate herself...unofficially."

Hartman smiled and nodded.

"Hmm. I haven't been to New York in a while. I think I might just take a trip."

One week later, Cole was sitting at the bar at Dos Caminos, a trendy, upscale Mexican restaurant in New York's SoHo district. The restaurant was a popular destination for the wealthy urban crowd that called SoHo home. This was the third evening he had camped out, nursing his Tecate beer and grazing on nachos and gourmet tacos. Cole knew that it would only be a matter of time before Paula Dorn would stop in for dinner. All New York's entertainment elite did.

He saw her enter through the front door with two girlfriends, all three decked out in the latest Paige Verdugo skinny jeans, trendy pumps and casual lace tops. The greeter immediately seated them in a booth in the room adjacent to the bar. Cole waited for them to get their drinks and place their orders. He finished his Tecate and casually walked over to where the trio was happily talking and laughing with no concern or awareness of their surroundings.

Cole sauntered up to the edge of their booth, produced his PI badge and announced, "Excuse me, ladies, and please pardon the interruption. My name is Cole Draper, Private Investigator, and I'd like to have a word with Ms. Dorn. It will only take a minute."

Stunned and a little annoyed, Paula Dorn sharply asked, "What's this about?"

"Yes, ma'am. Would you mind moving to another table with me so we can talk in private?"

"Not until I know what this is about."

"Yes, ma'am. It's about someone you once knew. Petty Officer Roger McLaren."

Paula Dorn's eyes widened and her skin turned pale. After a few seconds she turned her gaze away from Cole, and she stared at the bowl of chips in the middle of the table.

"I don't know what you're talking about," she said quietly.

Cole did not respond. There was silence as everyone at the table looked at Paula waiting for somebody to say something.

Paula's mind returned to that night thirty-six years ago, and the long-ago buried memory of what had happened played out like a surreal video.

She had just finished her shift as a waitress at the Ship's Cabin restaurant and returned to the small two-bedroom bungalow that she shared with McLaren. She hated her situation. McLaren was a son-of-a-bitch. He used her, but on her salary alone she couldn't afford a place for her and her sixteen-year-old sister, Michele, to live. McLaren gave them a roof over their heads. In return, Paula was his partner. She didn't enjoy it. Felt like a prostitute, but she had no other option. This was the best arrangement she could make, at least until Michele graduated from high school.

When Paula opened the door that evening, the first thing she heard was Michele crying and pleading, "Please stop!"

Paula rushed to the bedroom where a naked McLaren had forced Michele onto the bed. Michele was topless and McLaren was forcefully removing her shorts.

Paula jumped on McLaren as she yelled at him. "Stop it, you asshole!" She tried to pull him away from Michele, but he was too strong, and he pushed Paula off the bed and onto the floor.

"You'll get your turn," he shouted at Paula and turned his attention back to Michele.

Paula picked up a heavy brass plate that had been lying next to his uniform on the floor, swung it hard and hit McLaren on the back of his head. McLaren fell forward onto Michele.

Michele panicked, and was hyperventilating as she pushed his limp body off her and scrambled off the bed.

McLaren lay there, immobile with his eyes wide open and a trickle of blood dripping out of his mouth and nose.

Paula looked up from the table at Cole Draper and her two friends, and realized that she now had tears in her eyes. *How long have they been staring at me?*

"I knew this would happen one day," she calmly said and then talked for forty minutes non-stop.

"She recounted the entire story in front of me, and her very stunned friends," Cole explained to Heather while they sat on the deck of her new home overlooking the bay. "She and her sister buried McLaren on the beach that night. He had a little over ten-thousand dollars in cash that she thought he was going to use to buy a better car. She took that, and they packed all of his belongings in a U-Haul trailer, hitched it to his car and moved to a small apartment on Long Island. The lease on the cottage expired at the end of the month, and the real estate manager had been notified that the house would be vacated because McLaren was being transferred. So there was nothing left in the house to make anyone think that anything suspicious had happened. The house was clean. There was never any reason to try to find her."

"That's sad," lamented Heather. "What a terrible thing to have to live with all these years."

"Yeah. She said she was relieved to not have to carry that secret around any longer."

"Why didn't she just stay and tell the police what happened? It sounds justifiable to me."

"She was nineteen, scared, and didn't have any other family to turn to. Her biggest fear was what would happen to Michele if she had to go to jail."

"Do you think she will go to jail now?" asked Heather as she looked thoughtfully at the watery horizon.

Cole looked at the deck floor and moved his head slightly side to side. "I don't know. The police still don't have any hard evidence to link her to McLaren's murder. All we have is her confession to me that evening in New York. And you can bet that she's lawyer'd up by now. I just don't know."

THE TOWN HALL INCIDENT

By Patrick Clark

The large banner hanging from the railing in front of the East Beach Bay Front Club read, *Welcome Senator Scott Paige.*

"This must be the place," observed Agent Mark Dandridge of the Secret Service as he pulled his white Chevrolet Impala with U.S. Government license plates into the gravel spaces across the street.

"Nice location," replied his partner, Toni Estefan. She leaned forward in the passenger seat, looked to her left and scoped the brown single-story main building and tall observation tower. "Nice neighborhood, too. This shouldn't be too hard to prep for."

"Yeah, right," replied Dandridge as he turned to face her. "Were it not for the controversy over his comments on free trade, this would be a piece of cake. He upset a lot of people with that."

Agents Dandridge and Estefan were the lead agents

assigned to conduct a site survey to assess the potential threat and coordinate manpower and equipment requirements in advance of Presidential candidate Senator Scott Paige's planned town hall meeting at the Bay Front Club. The visit was planned for Monday afternoon, which left fewer than seventy-two hours for them to prepare for the arrival of the senator's campaign bus in East Beach.

Dandridge picked up his iPhone from the car's console pocket between the seats and opened a file in his notes app that referenced the assignment. He scrolled through the information until he found what he was looking for. "Our point of contact is the neighborhood association manager, name is Ted Gordon. It says here that the doors are always locked and only accessible with a key fob. And there is no door chime, so he recommends calling his cell phone when we arrive and he will meet us at the door."

Estefan opened the car door, and as she slid out of the front passenger seat remarked, "Okay. Why don't you do that? I'm going to take a look at the tower over here."

"Sure thing, Partner," he replied while he leaned forward to watch her exit.

With her left hand on the car top, Estefan dipped her head and looked back at him with an alluring smile as she closed the door with her right hand.

Dandridge poked the number provided into his phone as he slid out of the driver's seat and slipped into his blue sport coat before closing the car door. After speaking briefly with Gordon, he walked over and joined his partner as she strolled around the tower.

Estefan's tan skin tone and dark brown hair, which

she wore pulled back in a ponytail, were gifts from her Cuban parents. Her splendid physique was a result of her extreme fitness routine. Even wearing a very ordinary blue business pantsuit and blazer, which adequately hid her shoulder holster and Glock-42 sidearm, Estefan was a very attractive woman. *My partner ain't hard to look at*, thought Dandridge as he walked up and stood beside her.

"Look up there." Estefan looked skyward and pointed toward the 360-degree balcony of the tower. "The tower's going to have to be secured and a couple of agents will need to be stationed in there."

Dandridge turned toward a small park area to his left, which was surrounded by eight private homes, each with a third floor or higher observation room that, no doubt, provided wonderful views of the Chesapeake Bay. "Hell, that's not the only problem. Look at that." He drew her attention toward the lot of observation rooms.

Estefan scanned the area then made eye contact with Dandridge. "Shit."

"C'mon, let's go meet with Gordon," said Dandridge. "He's standing by the door."

"I'll be leaving now if that's okay, Jack."

"Yes, of course. I'll see you in the morning, Doris," replied Jack Taylor, President and CEO of Beach Tool and Die Company, as he sorted through his side desk drawer looking for a USB memory stick he had placed in there.

"Uhmm, no, you won't, Jack. Tomorrow is

Saturday."

"Yes, yes, of course." His face flushed and he wore a thin smile. "Saturday. I guess I'm a little distracted. Have a nice weekend, Doris. I'll see you on Monday."

"Jack, is everything alright?"

"Yes. Everything's fine. I'll be leaving soon, too. Thank you."

The door closed quietly as Doris, his longtime administrative assistant, left the office shortly after noon. Business at Taylor's Tool and Die Company wasn't as brisk as it once had been so Fridays were pretty quiet in the shop. There just were not enough orders to keep the shop humming for five full days each week. Much of his business had been lost to companies overseas, where labor was much less expensive.

Business had never been this bad in over three generations of the family's ownership. Only two years ago, the shop had enough work to keep two full shifts running, with each of the twenty-two machines fully operational. Then he lost one large contract to produce plastic ignition key parts for Ford and shortly after that, a smaller contract to produce toggle switches for Sikorsky Aircraft Company. In each case, he was underbid by foreign competition when the contract was recompeted. Now, he no longer had enough work to keep two full shifts running. Jack had to lay off two-thirds of his workforce and curtail the shop to one shift.

To compete with the lower priced competition, Jack purchased a high-end, 3-D printer that created objects out of carbon fiber from a computer-aided design in less time than his machine shop could. There was no additional machinery required. No machine set-up and no labor costs. He'd purchased the 3-D printer hoping to shave costs that could help secure more business. If it did, he planned to purchase several more 3-D printers. Unfortunately, he had no new business and now an additional $10,000 debt.

Jack knew from personal experience that objects he created on the printer were of equal or better quality than products that the laborers in his shop made. Over the last two weeks, after the shift workers had left the building, Jack had used the 3-D printer to manufacture parts using a schematic that he downloaded from the internet and saved on his USB memory stick.

"Hello, Mr. Gordon. I'm Agent Dandridge and this is my partner, Agent Estefan." Dandridge extended his hand in greeting. "This looks like a very nice neighborhood. Are all these homes new?"

"I guess that depends on your definition of new. They've all been built within the last ten years. Phase one opened in 2004 and we just started the final development phase of the community this year."

"Nice," replied Dandridge as he looked left and right down East Beach Drive and observed custom designed homes and manicured landscapes. "Very nice."

"Let me show you where the town hall meeting will take place," said Gordon, as he led them through the doorway and down the hall toward the main room. "We're pretty excited about this. It's an active community, so I'm sure there will be a pretty good crowd here. Some of the residents have said that they hope he'll stay for a bit and grip 'n' grin."

They entered the main hall of the clubhouse through the doorway at the back of the room, and the agents immediately scanned the area for vulnerabilities and emergency exits. From the vantage point of the hallway entrance, the left wall had a substantial fireplace flanked by two outside doorways. The wall directly in front of them had the most windows and faced sand dunes along the Chesapeake Bay and the beach area beyond the dunes. The right wall was windowed, faced the pool, and had one outside doorway leading to the pool deck.

"We thought the best place for the senator to stand would be over here," Gordon remarked from where he stood near the center of the far wall. He turned toward the agents and extended his arms to indicate the area. "The audience can be seated facing the windows. With the TV crews behind the audience, the senator's backdrop will be a panoramic view of the bay."

The agents exchanged glances and Dandridge spoke. "Sir, that would look nice, but I'm not sure we would be comfortable with that. Ordinarily, we like to have the protectees with their backs to something substantial, like the fireplace over there." Dandridge turned to face the fireplace. "That'll take one potential threat area out of the equation."

"Sure. Of course, whatever you think is best," replied Gordon.

"What we need to do, sir, is complete a site survey. We'll need to spend a few hours snooping around this building and the surrounding terrain. We may also want to look at some of the private residences nearby. Oh, and we will also need a copy of the neighborhood plat to look at. Can you help us with that?"

"Of course. Whatever you need."

"Sir," interjected Estefan, "after we complete our site survey, we'll develop a security plan. We'll coordinate that plan with you and with local law enforcement so that the event runs smoothly. We strive to be as non-disruptive to the community as possible, but the security of the protectee is the number one priority."

"Sure. I understand. I don't think there will be any problems in this neighborhood and I'll help any way I can," replied Gordon.

With Doris out of the office and the USB memory stick in hand, Jack stood up from behind his desk and walked through his office door, past Doris's U-shaped chocolate-colored desk and onto the main floor of his 10,000-square-foot machine shop. A variety of blue and gray metal lathes, milling machines, grinding machines, and jig grinders were arrayed in rows on the concrete floor according to size and manufacturing purpose. The shop was empty and silent and the lights turned off. The afternoon sun shone through the dark tinted windows and illuminated dust particles floating through the air, which gave the effect of a winter snowfall. The computer screens attached to each dormant machine produced an eerie blue glow.

It wasn't supposed to be like this. My business is failing because of cheaper foreign competition and I'm in debt up to my ears. My marriage is failing 'cause the business is failing. This is bullshit, and it's not my fault. He stood there for a few minutes and surveyed the scene, recalling better days. Small tears formed, and he fought the urge to scream in anger. *Dammit! I don't deserve this! Paige is wrong! Free trade has ruined my business!*

He felt his pulse intensify. The carotid artery in his neck throbbed and he heard the surge ring in his ears as he walked with long, purposeful strides toward the 3-D printer located on an aluminum desk behind a cubical in the left corner of the far wall.

The printer stood about a foot-and-a-half tall, two-feet wide and sixteen-inches deep. There was a roll of black carbon fiber filament on each side of the print nozzle that reminded him of a reel-to-reel tape machine like one he owned in the '70s. He pulled the roller chair out from under the desk and sat in front of the computer attached to the printer. As he had done every night for the last two weeks, he logged onto the computer, inserted the USB memory stick in the drive and moved his wireless mouse, clicking several times as he opened the file on the USB drive that showed all the schematic drawings of a Colt Mustang .38-caliber pocket-size handgun.

Dandridge and Estefan split up to conduct the site survey. Dandridge canvassed the private homes with second- and third-floor windows overlooking the grassy space where most of the crowd was expected to be, and where Senator Paige would probably walk through the crowd and shake the hands of potential voters. Estefan checked out the Bay Front Club building, including the observation tower and grassy dunes. The concern would be the small fitness center located adjacent to the pool, which offered a clear view through the windows to the spot where the senator would stand during the town hall question and answer session.

Just under four hours later, they met on the club deck that faced the Chesapeake Bay and sat in a shaded area on cherry-wood rocking chairs. Dandridge removed his sport coat and hung it over the back of his chair. He stretched his legs, interlocked his hands behind his head, and took in the view of the bay.

As partners, they had spent many hours in the gym together. Estefan admired his lean body and toned muscles. She watched him stretch and forced herself not to think about how handsome Dandridge was. She leaned toward him and spoke first. "The infrastructure doesn't look bad. I found a few vulnerabilities but we can manage them pretty easily. What did you find?"

"I think we need to get him inside the clubhouse quickly. Once inside, the audience will have been screened through the metal detector. He'll be safe there. My biggest concerns are the private homes. Any one of those around the open courtyard would give a shooter an ideal perch," he replied. He finished his stretch, turned, and now faced her. "Like you said, we can manage it, but it's going to require a pretty large team."

He leaned closer to Estefan and she caught him staring down the front of her blouse at the tops of her breasts.

She responded with a mischievous smile wide enough to make her cheeks pucker. "What's on *your* mind?" she asked.

"Right now? A big juicy cheeseburger."

Estefan controlled her urge to laugh at his obvious lie.

"Whadaya say we find someplace close, grab a bite to eat, and then head back to the office and lay out a plan," continued Dandridge, his face flush after being caught admiring her breasts.

"Sure," replied Estefan, followed by wide smile. *Shit,* she thought. *He knows I'm attracted to him and I know he's attracted to me. This could get very complicated.* With a wry smile, she raised herself out of the chair then continued, 'Let's go. I saw a place on Shore Drive called Cap'n something. The place looked packed so it must be good."

Dandridge rose out of his chair and announced, "Okay. Let's go."

The monitor on the 3-D printer in Jack's shop showed thirty-five seconds remained before the job would be complete. Jack watched every pass of the carbon-fiber cartridge as the blue light moved across the titanium platform. First to the left, then to the right, then back again. With each pass, the shape of the Colt Mustang pistol trigger mechanism grew more distinct.

Jack turned the monitor toward him so he could get a better look at the schematic on screen to compare it with the part that was being created. *It looks perfect. Just like the other components.*

After the last pass, he reached his blue leather-gloved hands into the printer, removed the part, and set it on the cold steel cooling platform. While the trigger cooled, he cleaned the small amount of carbon debris off the printer bed, leaving it as clean as when he'd started. Satisfied the job was complete, he rolled his chair back and looked over the workspace. He smiled a devious half-smile, which was reflected in the darkened screen of the sleeping computer. *That's it, Jack,* he thought as he looked at his image reflected on the monitor. *You have all the parts. Assemble it. Test it. Use it.*

With their food cravings fulfilled, Dandridge and Estefan returned to their temporary desks in the Secret Service office on Granby Street near the MacArthur Center. It was late on a Friday afternoon, and most of the local agents were gone for the day, with orders to return for a 10:00 a.m. meeting on Saturday to be briefed on the security plan and their individual assignments. They walked through the cubicle farm to the row of three offices with partial glass walls on the side of the building overlooking City Hall Avenue. The sun was low in the sky and shone brightly through the window of the Norfolk Field Service Director's office.

Dandridge knocked as he opened the door to her

office. "Director Hoffman. You have a few minutes so we can bring you up to date on what we found?"

"Sure do. I've been waiting for the two of you. Come in and have a seat."

Dandridge did most of the talking as they back-briefed Hoffman on the layout of the Bay Front Club, the neighborhood, and the senator's schedule. Hoffman listened intently and paid close attention to the neighborhood drawings that Dandridge had borrowed from Gordon. The briefing lasted about thirty minutes.

Hoffman stood and quietly walked over to the window. The sun was now almost gone. "You two are aware of the recent threats against Senator Paige?" She turned back to face Dandridge and Estefan. "The director over at Threat Assessments has informed me that the Internet hits on Paige have ratcheted up since he came out with his views on free trade. Many of them can be construed as threatening."

"Yes, ma'am," they replied in unison.

"Good. Can you have a plan ready for my approval by eight a.m. and be ready to brief assignments by ten?" she asked. "NPD, the Sheriff, and Fire and Rescue will have representatives there."

"We'll work all night if we have to," replied Dandridge as he looked at Estefan, knowing she would agree.

"That's right, Director. Whatever it takes," added Estefan.

"Good. Thank you," replied Hoffman as she walked behind her desk, sat down and returned to her computer email.

Dandridge turned toward Estefan and slightly cocked his head toward the door to indicate without words *we should leave now.*

The two agents quietly stood and walked out the door, Dandridge closing it behind them.

Dandridge and Estefan spent four-and-a-half hours preparing a detailed plan that was reviewed and approved by Hoffman at their 8:00 a.m. meeting, and then briefed the security teams. Their plan limited access to the secure area through establishment of a series of checkpoints to be manned by NPD and Sheriff Deputies. Secret Service agents were designated to patrol the area around the Bay Front Club and the private residences surrounding the open courtyard. K-9 detection support was included to clear the Bay Front Club prior to the senator's arrival and to troll the crowd that would likely assemble in the courtyard. Secret Service metal detectors were planned for the access points into the Bay Front Club. Finally, local hospitals with trauma centers were identified and emergency evacuation routes were established.

On Saturday and Sunday, physical barriers were erected at specified intersections leading into the East Beach neighborhood and a Secret Service mobile command post was delivered and tested to ensure that the communication center for the protective service was stable. The command center was needed to monitor any emergencies and to keep all participants in contact with one another. After a lively discussion, the agents agreed that Dandridge would take position as officer in charge at the command center and Estefan would take charge of the senator's protective detail.

A heavy weekend rain and a higher than normal flood tide—a result of a storm in the Atlantic—caused minor coastal flooding throughout Sunday night and through mid-morning on Monday. When Dandridge and Estefan arrived at East Beach at 9:00 a.m., NPD and sheriff's deputies were rearranging some of the orange and white traffic barriers that had been placed over the weekend and moved by the tidal floods. Estefan quietly looked through her open window on the passenger side of the black Secret Service Cadillac Escalade as they drove through numerous two- to four-inch puddles in the neighborhood.

Dandridge pulled into a gravel driveway between the Bay Front Club and two homes with garages facing the driveway. He parked behind the mobile command center that was already parked next to the Bay Front Club fitness room and a rack of brightly colored kayaks.

"This doesn't leave much room for the owners of these houses to park in their garages," remarked Estefan.

"Yeah, I know. They don't normally allow this, but Gordon talked to the owners and he assured me it won't be a problem," replied Dandridge. "This is a good spot. It's close to the venue, but out of the way." Dandridge turned and faced his partner before they stepped out of the Escalade. Without speaking, he reached over and touched the back of her hand.

Estefan rolled her hand over and held his for just a moment. They each sensed that their relationship had crossed a boundary between professional and personal, and pulled back. Estefan smiled and Dandridge noticed crescent shaped curves on her lower eyelids that accentuated her smile. They sat without speaking for a few moments, content that it felt right.

Doris arrived in the office late, just before 11:00 a.m., and was logging on to her computer when Brett Kluwer, the shop foreman and longtime friend, knocked on her door, then entered the office.

"Good morning, darlin'," he said cheerfully. "It's always good to see that beautiful smile on a Monday morning."

"Flattery, my good friend, will get you in trouble with HR these days," she replied, as she looked over the top of her Dell monitor and made eye contact with Brett.

"And since you're the HR department, my dear, I'll take that threat with the same serious intent with which it was delivered," he replied with a mischievous smile. "So, Jack appears to be running late this morning. What time do you expect him?"

"He probably won't be in today," replied Doris. "Jack sent in an application a few weeks ago and was selected to join the audience at Senator Paige's town hall meeting this afternoon. I think he'll just go straight there and then home afterward."

"Hmm," mumbled Brett. "He left this memory stick in the 3-D printer." He set the stick on Doris's desk. "I was hoping I could talk with him about it. I guess he must have been working on this over the weekend."

"Huh, that's odd." She leaned back in her chair, her lips tight and brow furrowed. "He usually tells me if he's going to work late or on the weekend."

Brett walked over and stood next to Doris and rested his knuckles on her desk. "Doris, this may seem like an odd question, but why d'ya suppose the boss would 3-D print, out of carbon fiber, all of the parts needed to assemble a handgun?"

"A handgun?" she answered in a voice at least one octave higher than normal. "That's odd."

"Yeah. Thought so, too."

"I have no idea why he would do that. We don't have any pending contracts for anything like that. None that I'm aware of, anyway."

After a brief pause, Doris made direct eye contact with him. "Are you sure about this?" she asked.

"Yeah. I looked at the file on the stick. It's a schematic of every part needed to assemble a Colt thirty-eight caliber. When I saw he printed a trigger mechanism on Friday, I looked back in the computer memory to see what else he might have printed. Doris, he has definitely printed every part needed to assemble a gun."

Doris raised herself out of her chair and Brett stepped back to give her space as she walked toward Jack's closed office door. She started to reach for the door handle, then stopped, and with moist eyes, turned back to face him.

"Brett, I've been worried about Jack lately. He seems to be getting very depressed. And, he's been distracted a lot lately." Her lips started trembling as she continued, "I'm afraid he may use the gun on himself."

Brett leaned his backside against Doris's desk and gripped the table with both hands and stared at the floor. He exhaled hard through his nose and said, "That really doesn't make sense. If he wanted to do that, why not just get a real gun? Why build one from carbon fiber?"

Doris started to walk back toward Brett, and was about to reply that she didn't know why.

In a sudden powerful motion, he pushed off the desk and faced her. "Shit!" he exclaimed. Brett clasped his hands behind his head and began to pace. "Shit!" he repeated.

"What? What is it?" Doris moved to intercept him and stand face-to-face.

"Dammit." He paused briefly before continuing. "A weapon made out of carbon fiber will not be detected by a metal detector."

It took a moment for Doris to understand what Brett had just suggested and the realization hit her like a heavyweight boxer's right hook. She felt lightheaded and steadied herself by leaning on her desk. As she turned to lean on her desk, Brett moved with her to make sure she didn't fall. Doris placed her left hand on Brett's shoulder and raised her right hand to cover her mouth.

Tears started to well up as she made eye contact with Brett. "Oh my God. Do you really think he would do that? Do you really think he would try to shoot Senator Paige? Why would he do that?"

"I don't know. I hope I'm wrong but it's the only explanation I have."

Doris stood and started to walk around her desk to where the telephone was located. "I'll call him on his cell phone and—"

"No, Doris," interrupted Brett. "We need to call the police."

Jack left his home in Chesapeake early, stopping at McDonald's for a breakfast burrito and a cup of coffee. He arrived at the Bay Front Club two hours before Senator Paige was scheduled to arrive, as recommended in the brochure that accompanied his letter of invitation to the campaign town hall meeting. This would allow sufficient time for check-in, seating, and a briefing of the meeting rules presented by a representative of the Norfolk League of Women Voters. He parked in a lot near a waterfront restaurant and was shuttled on a golf cart to the Bay Front Club by volunteers. He took his place in line behind a slightly bald, well-dressed man in a grey suit. He surveyed the others in line ahead of him and felt comfortable with his choice of grey slacks and blue blazer. *Great. I'll fit in easily with this crowd*, he thought. *I don't want to bring any undue attention to myself.* He also wore a calf holster and his carbon-fiber .38 under his right pant leg.

The line was on the outside deck of the clubhouse and moved toward a table where two volunteers checked in the invitees. Past the check-in table was a metal detector like the ones in use at most airports. Beyond that there was only one open door to the meeting room. The remaining doors were all closed and guarded by sheriff's deputies.

A man struck up a conversation with Jack about the venue, which they both agreed was perfect for this occasion.

When Jack reached the check-in table, he faced an attractive woman he estimated to be in her early forties with strawberry blond hair. Her nametag read *Linda, East Beach Volunteer.*

"Hello, sir. Welcome to the campaign town hall Meeting. Can I see your driver's license, please?"

"Of course." Jack pulled his wallet out of his back pocket, removed his license, and handed it to Linda.

With his identity verified on the invitee list, Jack was told to remove all metal items from his pockets, remove his belt and shoes, and proceed through the metal detector, which he did very deliberately. *Don't forget anything*, he thought. *Don't blow this.*

Jack placed his wallet, cell phone, belt, and tie clasp in a small tray and handed that and his shoes to an NPD officer before he was gestured to walk through the detector. He took a deep breath, stepped through to the other side, and did not set off the alarm. *Nothing. I'm clear*, he thought. *I made it.* Relieved to have made it through the one check point that could have caused his plan to fail, Jack picked up his shoes and stepped toward the meeting room. He stopped when he felt the touch of the NPD officer on his shirtsleeve.

"Sir. Excuse me, sir."

Oh shit. Jack's breath quickened, and his pulse pounded in his throat.

"You forgot your items, sir."

Jack turned to face the officer who was pointing at the tray on the table next to the detector.

"I think you'll need those," the officer prodded him.

"Yes. Yes. I'm sure I will." Jack picked up the tray. "Thank you."

"No problem, sir."

Jack collected his things, slipped on his belt and shoes and entered the meeting room. There were six rows of folding chairs. Each row had twelve chairs that were arranged in an arc facing the podium. The moderator's chair was placed in the center, facing the podium. Television news cameras were set up in the back of the room and microphones were hung from the ceiling.

The group entered in single file, and each person was presented with a folder filled with political pamphlets from a league representative. Jack took a seat in the second row, two seats in from the right, next to the slightly balding man he had talked to while in line.

"Are you excited about this?" the man asked.

"Yes. Very. I have waited months for this opportunity."

Dandridge and Estefan were waiting on the clubhouse deck when Senator Paige's campaign bus stopped in front of the Bay Front Club with the distinctive *pshuss* sound of the compressed air brakes. The bus door opened, and the agents stepped inside to greet the senator, provide a short brief on the security arrangements and introduce Estefan as the lead agent for the detail.

When the brief was completed, Dandridge emerged first and walked around the side of the clubhouse to take his station in the command center and establish communication over the secure wireless system. The communication system included a common channel, as well as separate channels for Secret Service agents, EMT and the NPD and sheriff's deputies. Satisfied that he had clear communication with all of the agencies, Dandridge notified Estefan that all elements of the protective operation were ready.

Jack heard the commotion outside as Senator Paige emerged from the bus and was greeted by cheers from a crowd of supporters. A petite, middle-aged woman with short brown hair and a grey tweed business suit approached the podium and spoke into the microphone.

"Ladies and gentlemen, my name is Carol Middleton, and on behalf of the Norfolk League of Women Voters, I want to thank you for participating in this presidential election town hall meeting. Please join me in welcoming Senator Scott Paige."

The audience stood and politely applauded as Senator Paige entered the room from the hallway. He was five-foot eight-inches, much shorter than Jack anticipated. He had a full head of grey hair and wore a blue suit, white shirt and red tie.

Jack looked at the people around him, and when he was certain the attention of the audience was directly on the senator as he approached the podium, Jack dropped his folder on the floor. He bent over to pick it up, and in one swift move snatched the handgun from his leg holster and slipped it into his pocket. *Two shots are all I'll need. One for him and one for me.*

In the command center, Dandridge watched the monitors from three television stations as well as the video feed set up by the Secret Service technicians. Senator Paige entered the room. Dandridge saw the three agents in position with Estefan closest to the podium, the second agent in the back of the room, and the third next to the exit door to the left of the podium.

Senator Paige was presenting his opening remarks when the direct phone line from Director Hoffman pulsated loudly.

"Agent Dandridge, this is Hoffman. I've received calls from VBPD and NPD. We've confirmed a tip from a valid source. We have credible intelligence that there is a shooter in the room. Evacuate the protectee. Acknowledge."

Goddammit! "Understood. There is a shooter in the room."

He pressed a button on the console and activated the Secret Service-only line to alert the agents. "This is Dandridge. There is a shooter in the room. Evacuate the senator. Repeat. Evacuate the senator."

Estefan made eye contact with the other two agents as the three of them began to converge toward the senator. She spoke into her wrist microphone. "Confirmed. We are evacuating."

Something's happening, thought Jack as he saw three people move quickly toward the senator. NPD officers entered the room through the two doors in front of him. He glanced around the room. *Dammit!* Beads of sweat formed on his forehead. *They must have found out! Dammit!* Others in the audience began to stand up. Jack's pulse was pounding so hard he felt like his head would explode. He pulled the handgun out of his pocket, aimed it at the senator and shouted, "Senator Paige!"

He made eye contact with Senator Paige and then pulled the trigger twice before the slightly bald man sitting next to him tackled him. Jack pulled the trigger again as they fell to the floor, and a third round went harmlessly into the ceiling.

From the monitor in the control room, Dandridge watched as the detail closed in on the senator. People in the audience stood up. Some started to move toward the exits and blocked the agents' approach to Senator Paige. Dandridge saw Estefan move toward the senator and around the moderator. He saw her look over her shoulder toward the man in the grey slacks and blue blazer before she fell forward into the podium. *Oh God. Toni's been shot.*

He watched the other two agents escort the senator out of the room, his feet barely touching the floor, to the Secret Service SUV waiting outside.

Through his headphones he heard, "Agent Down! Estefan is down!"

Dandridge sat next to Estefan's hospital bed in the Critical Care Unit of Bayside Hospital after her surgery. He wore a yellow surgical gown over his clothes.

Estefan's eyes blinked several times as the anesthesia wore off. Her hand was in his latex-gloved hand when she awoke.

"Hi," he said with a reassuring smile.

The *puchung…puchung* sound of the respirator and rhythmic beeping of the heart-rate monitor were the only sounds in the room when Dandridge noticed her lips moving. He leaned closer to try to hear her.

"Ms. Estefan. Please don't try to speak," scolded the young registered nurse. "You're on a respirator, you have a breathing tube down your throat, as well as a chest tube to drain the fluid out of your lung." She held Estefan's other hand, and smiled to help ease the fear she anticipated from her new patient. "My name is Lara and I'm going to take care of you. You're going to be all right."

Estefan's eyes were now wide open and focused directly at Dandridge. Her face was pale and she began to shiver.

Lara handed an alphabet card and a small white board to Dandridge. "Ms. Estefan, if you want to communicate you can point to the letters on the card he is holding and spell out the words, or you can write on this white board with these markers. Can you do that?"

Toni nodded to indicate that she could and with a shaky hand began to point at letters on the alphabet card. She spelled out, *Was I shot?*

"You were," replied Dandridge warmly.

She spelled, *The shooter?*

"In custody."

Estefan's hand steadied and the tension in her face eased. She reached for the white board and marker, which Dandridge handed to her.

How did he get a gun in the room? she scribbled.

"It was made from carbon fiber."

Wrinkles appeared on her forehead and she wrote, *What?*

"It's a long story."

She quickly wiped the white board clean and then wrote, *The senator?*

"He's fine. He came here after it happened and stayed in the waiting room with me until you were out of surgery. I think he was genuinely concerned."

Nice to know. Her writing became easier. *I still won't vote for him, though.*

"I know. You don't like his positions on energy and

the environment."

They sat, just holding hands while Lara checked her vital signs and administered medication.

After a short time, Estefan picked up the white board again. *How am I?* she wrote.

"You were hit twice in the back. Both rounds punctured your left lung. The surgeon said you'll be fine, though. You'll just need someone to take care of you while you heal and rehab."

You?

Dandridge noticed her eyes open a little wider and saw her attempt to smile in spite of the tube in her throat. "Yeah. Definitely," replied Dandridge. Then he kissed her forehead.

SECOND CHANCE
AT EAST BEACH

By Michelle Davenport

Sometimes The Fates give you a second chance at life.
It's up to you to take that chance.
The Fates won't force your hand,
But can, on special occasions, lend you a helping hand.

Rick Dandes stared down at the business card being held out to him and frowned. "So there's nothing the doctors can do for my mother?" He watched the nurse sitting across from him, hoping she would tell him what he wanted to hear. He and his wife had just moved his mother into the cottage next to them in East Beach. He wanted to hear there was an easy fix, a pill that might make it all better, but somehow he knew she wouldn't give him that answer.

"Mr. Dandes, your mother doesn't need a doctor. She's not sick. Call the number I've given you. They can help." She urged him to take the card. "I've given them all the pertinent information, and they assure me that they can handle your case." The nurse raised her hand when he looked to argue. "Just do as they tell you and things will look much better."

In the corner, unseen, a shadowy figure glared at the nurse.

Three days later, Rick Dandes sat on his front porch, enjoying the gentle bay breeze and listening to a local baseball game. He still could not believe the conversation he'd had with the woman from the agency whom he had called at the nurse's suggestion. Now he was waiting for the young woman assigned to care for his mother to arrive.

A small convertible pulled up in front of the house, and a woman quickly got out. "Mr. Dandes." She approached him smiling. "I'm Stella from Second Chances."

For the first time in months, Rick smiled and felt a huge sense of relief. "Thank you for coming out so soon. I hope you can help Mom. If you'll follow me, I'll take you next door to my mother's house. You'll be living there with her."

They walked across the yard and up the steps to the wide porch of a cute sky-blue cottage. White shutters and gingerbread trim made the house worthy of a Coastal Living magazine cover. All of this, just a block away from the Chesapeake Bay. Stella took a deep breath and smiled.

This could be a great assignment.

"Mom?" Rick called out as he and Stella entered the cottage. He closed the door behind them.

Stella walked further into the open space that combined living room, dining room, and kitchen. She glanced about. Boxes sat waiting to be unpacked, and a woman sat listlessly staring out of the window. In the corner, Stella saw a shadowy figure. She narrowed her eyes and shook her head. *It can't be.*

"Mrs. Dandes." Stella spoke softly as she approached the woman. "Your son has told me all about you, and I hope you don't mind that he wants me to stay the summer with you."

Dorothy Dandes glanced at her son with suspicion, and Stella quickly sat down on the ottoman in front of her.

"I know what you're thinking, but I'm not a babysitter. I'm a helper. Who's going to do the heavy lifting for all the projects I'm sure you have around here? Your son?" Stella jerked her thumb in his direction. "He's going to be of no use. Have you met a man yet who can choose paint worth a darn? Or get those chores done in a timely manner?"

Dorothy chuckled as her son started to stutter. He quieted down at the slight shake of Stella's head.

"What do you say, Mrs. Dandes? Want a roommate for the summer?"

Rick and Stella watched the older woman, and

eventually she gave a small smile, and nodded her head.

"Fantastic!" Stella gave a small grin in Mr. Dandes' direction.

"How are you at painting?" Dorothy Dandes leaned forward, looking a bit more animated.

"I'm pretty good at wielding a brush," Stella said. "Do you know what colors you want to paint the rooms?"

Dorothy nodded her head.

"Then I say we go to Sherwin Williams. There's one just down the street. After we find paint and brushes and drop clothes and everything else we'll need, we'll go to dinner. Are you hungry?"

Dorothy shrugged.

"Once we get our supplies, I think we should stop at Cap'n Groovy's for a bite to eat. You're so lucky to be living in this area. There's so much around! We'll have to explore once we've got the place the way you want it."

The shadowy form slowly faded from view.

Mr. Dandes leaned over and kissed his mom's head. "Don't overdo it, Mom. And be sure to wear a light jacket. It's still chilly out there."

As he left, Dorothy peppered Stella with questions about her cooking abilities.

That's how the summer started for the Dandes family. Wherever you saw Dorothy, Stella was close by. They took long walks throughout the East Beach community, stopping to chat with new friends on the porches that were situated close to the sidewalk. If they weren't out walking and chatting with neighbors, they were at the pool, or going for a drive in Stella's convertible, or Dorothy was teaching Stella how to cook. They were a duo that seemed inseparable.

Dorothy bloomed in the community. She joined a book club and a gardening club. "Social butterfly" was the term that came to Rick's mind. He hadn't seen his mother this happy or busy since his father had passed away just last year.

He wished he could say the same for his wife. Her government contract had come to an end, and she seemed to be at loose ends. She'd said she wasn't sure if she wanted to continue working, and he had assured her that he would support her no matter what she decided. Yet, she'd still looked like something was bothering her.

She seemed to perk up and become more involved with the community when she started going on walks with Stella and his mother. He was quite pleased. Even better, she and his mother were getting along. They were finally bonding. More often than not, his mother and Stella joined Anna and him for dinner. Conversation revolved around what one or the other had found out about East Beach, or something that they wanted to do. One night it was about which flowers would best accent the pastel color of the home. Another night it was the controversy of the book club choosing to read *Fifty Shades of Gray*. Rick loved how animated his wife and mother were.

Rick pulled into the garage and grabbed the wine he had picked up on the way home. He smiled as he walked through the courtyard between the garage and his house. The aroma of lasagna gently wafted over him. The rich tomato smell mingled with the scents of garlic and fresh bread, and made his stomach growl. His wife and mother had decided to start making meals together, which worked well for him. Anna wasn't much of a cook, but with his mother's help, she was improving.

"Dinner was fantastic, ladies." Rick said with a sigh, as he mopped up the last of the marinara sauce with a crust of bread.

Stella started to clear the table, and shook her head at Dorothy and Anna. "You two stay put. You cooked, so I'll clean."

Anna cleared her throat. "Rick…" She paused, biting her lower lip. "I know things have been a bit out of whack since my contract ran out, but I've been thinking." She glanced at her mother-in-law to get a reassuring nod. "I don't want to try to renew my contract. I want to stay at home."

"That's fine, honey." Rick smiled at his wife, relieved that she had finally told him what was bothering her. "You know I'll support you in any decision you make." Rick jumped slightly when his mother popped him on the shoulder. "Hey, what was that for?"

"She wasn't finished, you dolt. Stop interrupting." Dorothy smiled at her daughter-in-law. "Go on, dear."

"Well, Rick, I want to stay at home for our children." Anna smiled at her husband as if she'd just given him a wonderful gift.

Rick sputtered slightly. "Well sure, honey. We can talk this over and..."

Dorothy rolled her eyes and Anna slumped slightly.

"Mr. Dandes, I don't think this is up for discussion." Stella said, as she served coffee.

Dorothy and Anna both laughed.

"What?" Rick asked.

Anna placed her hands on her stomach and began rubbing in small, comforting circles. "I'm pregnant," she said."

Rick sat in his chair, stunned.

The three women cast worried glances at each other.

"Honey, please say something," Anna pleaded.

A heartbeat later, Rick was out of his chair and hugging his wife. "Are you okay? When are you due? We need to get a crib!" He took a deep breath and grinned. "I'm rambling, aren't I?"

Everyone laughed. "Yes, but that's okay," Anna assured him, and gave him a kiss on the cheek.

Stella smiled and looked around. Finally, that pesky shadow had stopped following Dorothy around. Her job here was done.

The next morning, Rick came upon Stella packing up her car. "Are you going somewhere?"

Stella smiled. "My job is done, Mr. Dandes."

Rick shook his head. "But your contract is for the summer and it's only mid-August."

Stella smiled slightly. "The contract was for as long as your mother needed me. She doesn't need me anymore." She held up her hand to ward off any arguments. "If you'll look at your contract, Mr. Dandes, you'll see that it says for the entire summer or until the client no longer needs me. And your mother is listed as the client."

Rick helped Stella finish loading her car. "How did you know?"

"Know what, Mr. Dandes?"

"What my mother needed? When it was time to go? Any of it?" Rick cocked his head to the side, waiting.

"How I knew? I asked your mother. She lost her spouse and felt that she had no purpose. So I got her involved in your community. How I know she doesn't need me?" Stella chuckled. "She has a grandbaby on the way. I think she has plenty on her plate now."

Grinning at the thought of the new baby, Rick could only nod. He closed the car door for Stella as she buckled her seatbelt.

"Makes sense, doesn't it? Everyone needs to feel needed, and your mother now has that second chance. Good bye, Mr. Dandes."

Stella started her car and headed toward Shore Drive.

"Laying it on a bit thick, don't you think, Stella?"

Stella glanced over at the robed figure now

occupying her passenger seat. She knew no one else could see him, but it still creeped her out. "Sometimes you have to be a bit dramatic to get through to some people."

"If you'd only tip the hand in my favor, I could *so* make it worth your while."

"We've had this discussion, Hades. I work for The Fates. I go in to help, but not to make things go one way or the other. So give it a rest."

Stella shook her head as the robed figure growled and then disappeared.

"Some people never learn."

I HAVE A DRESS

By Karen Harris

The small, pewter frame caught a glimmer of sunlight as I held it near the window. The early morning light had been tepid, and the waters of the Chesapeake Bay, flat and indifferent. Now, as the haze began to dissipate, the landscape came alive. Beach-goers casually removed their sandals as they stepped from the tufted grass onto the cool sand. A light breeze friskily teased waves close to shore. Sea gulls were lurking near picnickers, eyeing their leftovers.

I slowly paced the waterfront terrace of the Bay Front Club, early for a rendezvous with long-time navy friends. Once a year, one of the couples hosted this walk down memory lane, as we poured over our pictures and mementos of our shared and varied histories. Retirement and East Beach had not been on my radar, not at all, when that photo was taken.

Stepping inside, I moved close to the stone hearth of the clubhouse, setting the photo on a small table. Sinking into a comfortable chair, I felt the years sliding away, the memories washing over me.

"What are you doing Saturday?" Jane asked the moment I picked up the phone.

"Nothing. Why don't you come to dinner with Cindy and me?" Cindy was my best friend and roommate.

"The *ball* is Saturday. Do you still want to go?"

I paused a moment, conjuring the memory of our conversation from the summer. The U.S. Navy Ball, I suddenly remembered. Jane and her pal, Mary, had bemoaned the expense of formal gowns and shoes as the price of dating their boyfriends. Both were seeing naval officers who were stationed in nearby Alameda. "I have a dress..." I had piped up. No navy beau, no thought of balls, just a dress from an old friend's wedding that spring. Apparently, Jane had taken those four words to heart. All these months later, with Mary long gone home to New York and medical school, Jane had thought of that gown and me.

The dress was a story in itself. An old friend from grade school, living four hundred miles away, had asked me to be a bridesmaid in her May wedding. I had been delighted. The sewing pattern had come in the mail and my mother, who had sewn costumes and other clothes for me, decided not to tackle the tricky taffeta herself. She had used the services of a professional seamstress on occasion, and I soon found myself standing before a tiny Portuguese woman. She assessed my underweight frame and set to work. During the final fitting, she declared, "The ruffle and bow are only lightly sewn, so they can be removed, and the horsehair binding will give it the finish of a ball gown." I had nodded and smiled, never imagining myself attending anything grander than the upcoming nuptials. Spending two years at a primarily agricultural university had only lowered my sartorial standards even further than my stylish mother could believe possible. However, here was Jane, awaiting my answer regarding the ball.

"Um, yes?" I managed.

Jane was off and running. "I think your date will be Greg's roommate." Greg was her boyfriend of two years, stationed on a nuclear-powered cruiser. "His name is Clay. We'll have drinks before the ball at Greg's and then on to the hotel. I'll call you later this week with the details. It will be a blast!"

I stood for a moment, phone in hand, looking out over the office. Cherry, a file clerk, caught my eye and came into my cubicle. "You look surprised," she said. "What's up?"

"I just..." I faltered. "I am going to the ball, the Navy Ball." It sounded so funny, I almost laughed. Bemused, that's what I was. And charmed, and taken aback. Balls were for fairy tales, or the debutantes in the newspaper. An anachronism in this modern city, this Baghdad-by-the-Bay.

The word would spread quickly and my staff would be pumping me for every detail as the week progressed. I loved working with this group of women. They were like a family and treated me with a kindness that I deeply appreciated.

But now, work and chat had to wait. The dress. I had to call Mom. It would have to be pressed and the ruffle and bow removed. Should I drag out the dyed-to-match shoes? What about jewelry? Maybe Cindy would have a thought about that. She was my roommate and closest friend. It was like living with Lucille Ball. She was smart, well-read, opinionated, and the funniest person I had ever known. She also had a great sense of style and loved a project. I knew I needed all the help I could get to be ready in only a few days.

As I had guessed, Cindy took charge as soon as we were home from our jobs. She marched me down the few blocks to Union Square's fashionable shops. Within forty-eight hours, long, white gloves were draped over our wicker love seat, with a pair of stylish black pumps resting beneath them. We carefully looked over her grandmother's crystal necklace for any loose beads. Cindy's new hairdresser cut my straight, brown hair into a soft bob, complementing my narrow face, with fringed bangs to frame my blue eyes.

We invited Jane to come to dinner on Wednesday, to glean information about my blind date. "So, what's he like?" Cindy asked as we tucked into roasted chicken.

"He is tall and blonde." Jane offered. "He seems really nice." She had only met him twice, and had little to impart.

I felt oddly removed from the conversation. This week had taken on a dreamy quality, and details seemed likely to awaken me, perhaps rudely. I was not comfortable with dating, like the rest of my friends seemed to be. I had put all of my energy into the preparations, and given almost no thought to the man with whom I would be spending the evening.

It soon emerged that Greg and Clay had also fed Jane, with an eye to learning more about me! She had only slightly more to tell them. Mary, our mutual friend, had been a work-mate of Cindy's and mine for a few months before her move home. The four of us had seen a movie or two, and had dined together a few times. Once alone, Jane had joined us for a meal and some shopping on a couple of occasions.

Saturday dawned with a dense fog covering the City by the Bay. Cindy and I dressed warmly and headed to the Marina to watch the Parade of Ships as they passed through the Golden Gate heading for the piers of San Francisco. The ubiquitous flock of pelicans flew by, glancing at the gathering crowds, seeking handouts. Their formation seemed to mimic the long-anticipated Blue Angels, drawing some laughter. Soon it became evident the fog was not going to lift, canceling the air show for the day. The crowd trickled away as soon as the last navy vessel passed Chrissy Field's lawn. We joined the uphill throng, stopping only to buy hotdogs from a street vendor, as we returned to our small apartment.

Our four-room domicile was as far removed as one could imagine from the elegance of the East Beach neighborhood where I recounted these momentous days. We had elected to use the front room as a living room, sharing the larger space off the kitchen as our bedroom. The Ritz, it was not. And then there were the charming women on the corner across the street.

Only four blocks from Union Square, our building was on the cusp of the Tenderloin, an ironic name for so rough an area, and just too far down the hill to be considered part of the tony Nob Hill set. The callbox at the entrance did not always send the calls up to our top-floor apartment. Homeless men sometimes gathered on our front steps, awaiting the bicycle messengers who would give them access to the roof for a safe night's sleep. The evenings brought out the prostitutes in their short skirts and skimpy coats.

Amazingly, Greg and Clay had an apartment only four blocks up the hill from ours, off the same cross street. They were on the much more fashionable California Street, firmly ensconced atop Nob Hill. Clay was to walk down to escort me to their apartment for the pre-ball party. The officers from his ship, and their dates, would gather there. A quick cable-car ride, and we would be at the gala.

"What if the buzzer is broken again?" I had wondered aloud, midweek.

"No problem. I can wait for him on the stoop. Anyway, you should make an entrance. I'll bring him up, put him in the living room, and then, ta-da, you come out of the bedroom and knock his socks off!" Another wrinkle ironed out by my fairy godmother.

Now, with Clay's arrival imminent, Cindy zipped me into the dress, and set out my shoes, holding me steady as I stepped into them. I stood, breathless, as she fastened the multiple strands of Austrian crystals. We gazed into the tiny bathroom mirror, amazed at the transformation

"Like a princess," I breathed. "I think I am going to

cry."

"You're ugly, Joyce. You'll always be ugly." Grinning, she intoned a line from a Dr. Demento song. Leave it to Cindy to make me smile.

One quick hug, and she swept out of the room and down to the stoop to wait for Clay. I was left to my own thoughts for the first time in days. Truly, I was more excited than nervous. The ball, with its local dignitaries, traditions, dinner, and dancing offset any concerns I had about whether my date would like me, or I him. For a worrywart like me, this was exhilarating.

I heard the click of the lock as they entered. Once they stepped into the living room, I made my entrance. My gown was royal blue, now strapless, held up by its stay-filled bodice, while the skirt swayed satisfactorily at the slightest movement. The ballet-length complemented my height and the long white gloves gave me an elegance I felt proud to borrow. The crystal necklace finished the ensemble better than any jewels could have.

And there he stood. *Not tall, not really blond*, ran quickly through my mind. Clay was my height, and his hair was a sandy brown. His eyes were green, and his smile slightly shy and boyish. We must have introduced ourselves, but that moment is lost to me now. He seemed as shy as I felt just then. Cindy posed us and took a photograph of this first, old-fashioned and tentative moment.

That small portrait, of a young officer and his slightly nervous

date, rested comfortably in my hand as I recalled those long ago events. What if I had never mentioned the dress to Jane? What if Mom had made the dress instead? What if the seamstress had never mentioned repurposing the bridesmaid gown? Or, what if I had never been asked to be in that wedding? Sometimes, one's fate seems to change in an instant. Or a series of instants.

As I gazed across the Chesapeake, my mind's eye saw the sparkling San Francisco Bay, and the Blue Angels flying over the Golden Gate the day after the ball. I could still feel my heart's quickening beat as Clay took my hand for the first time, later that afternoon, as we came across a Columbus Day parade on our way back from watching the flying aces.

Now, as Clay, my husband of thirty years, stepped through the glass doors of the Bay Front Club to join me, the photo caught his eye and his knowing smile mirrored mine.

.

LIGHTS ON WATER

By Will Hopkins

During the summer of 1952, people across America reported seeing strange lights in the night skies. These sightings peaked that July, most notably along the Eastern Seaboard. The lights have never been explained.

Plink.

The little tin cap bounced on the porcelain tiles, executed a perfect edge-flip and rolled into the adjoining stall.

Sigh.

Harry Bynde listened as the tiny knurls rattled across the floor, popping against grout lines like rifle cracks inside the men's room. The cap finally made the far wall and died.

Harry held his breath a few beats. Nothing except for the whirring window fan propping the raised sash. He gently slipped the chromed catch and peered out of the stall. The other stall doors yawned half-open at empty washbasins along the opposite wall. Harry clicked his fingers, pocketed the pint, and strode to the nearest basin, where he opened the faucet like he meant business while necking around to check for foot shadows beneath the hallway door. As Harry caught only a soft glow of polished wax, he poured the last inch of hooch into his mug and deposited the bottle in the bin, covering the Royal Russian eagles with a wad of paper towels.

Harry made the mistake of checking the mirror. Christ. He'd forgotten to shave this morning. He studied himself for a moment under the buzzing florescent lights. Weary eyes, gruff stubble and a pincushion of paunch now showing along the forty-two-year-old jaw. He leaned in and hazed the image with a huff of vodka-heated breath. Off spun the water, up went the mug and out went Harry through the heavy mahogany door onto barristers' row at the old Norfolk firm of Buckman, Marlow, and Orange.

Harry passed down the corridor concluding that nothing had changed in the last fifteen billable minutes. George Lattimer still hunched over a casebook, pipe in mouth, pencil poised to make some note on a blank legal pad. In the next office, L. Steven Roth, Esq., the firm's domestic man, did his best to console a fledgling divorcee. She had a nice set of legs. *Stevie might take this one pro bono*, Harry surmised. The next three big-window offices sat empty. Old man Adams and Junior were stuck in court all day. Orange was still vacationing in Nags Head.

Harry dipped into his small office, gently shut the pebble glass door, and plopped behind the antique (i.e., second-hand) walnut desk. He'd pulled the window blinds tight against the afternoon sun, cooling the room in gray-green shadow. Except for the desk, where a lamp burned away at four forest green files stacked atop the stained blotter. *Too bad they hadn't evaporated like some noxious chemicals during the latrine call,* Harry thought. Coiled around them were bound copies of *Annual Reports* from the State Bureau of Highways and Roads, and a dog-eared *Mechanic's Guide to Hudson Automobiles, Model Years 1948-1952.* Harry's notes, phone records, pencils, and candy wrappers littered the remaining space; while just at the limit of the ellipse of light a trick dodo bird bobbed up and down into a glass of water, flicking reflections across the morning paper. *Air Force at Loss to Explain Unusual Objects* read the headline along the edge of the fold. A stock shot of an F-94 rocketed above the two-column story. *Join the club, boys,* Harry thought, considering how Adams expected at least one Hudson case to be settled or docketed for trial by Labor Day.

"Yes, yes, Harry," Adams had said, bobbing his slick-silvered head like the damn dodo. "There's gold in there, my boy. Simply need to apply yourself, just like the old days. Yes, that's the spirit. Fine, fine. Now how's that chicken?" That had been at the Memorial Day picnic.

Harry squeaked back in the sprung chair and watched the ceiling fan revolve sleepily overhead. He circled through the situation. Again. Four late-model Hudson sedans had crashed in Virginia during the last thirteen months. No apparent reason, though the drivers reported losing steering control just before the crash (okay, maybe he'd suggested that to three of the potential plaintiffs). Five injured, one dead—a young mother of three. Harry had traded a bottle of rye for some basic statistical analysis by a friend who taught eleventh-grade math at Maury High. The chance of these wrecks happening out of the blue was approximately 1,288,000 to 1. Even Harry's lazy legal mind had recognized the lush pickings if he got those numbers before a jury. Five to ten grand for the cripples, minimum of twenty for each of the three poor kids and the grieving husband. Now multiply that by 33%, plus the incidental research costs and fees, etc., etc.

Harry, however, had one small problem, to wit: three of the cars were long gone—junked and melted for scrap steel—while the remaining car sat on blocks in a backyard over in Portsmouth, sans the suspect front end which the owner had removed in order to turn the lousy heap into a hotrod V8. Harry needed some evidence of defect. Even better, something physical and real, that jurors could heft and feel dangerous in their hands before passing it down the box. He nursed the warm two-dollar vodka and watched the fan.

The bang of the dumpster truck three stories down startled him awake. A slat of light leaking through the blinds sliced across the electric wall clock. Two-forty. Before the fan made another turn, he jolted up in the chair.

"That's it!"

Harry drained the mug into a potted rubber plant on the radiator, grabbed his jacket, and made for the door.

Paula, the receptionist, balanced the phone on her shoulder, working an emery board across a nail. She glanced up when Harry tossed a tented business card on her desk. He breezed on, tapping at his watch and mouthing "out." He'd printed *Client Meeting - Important* on the back of the card. She rolled her eyes and went back to her afternoon phone conversation.

"Yeah, sorry. Just one of them leaving early. Uh huh. That one. So who—"

Harry shouldered the heavy bronze door and stepped out in the July sun. He shielded his eyes and made for the car lot across the street. He was already sweating by the time he climbed inside the sun-broiled Mercury Montclair. He was barely making payments on the heap. A parking ticket stuck to the windshield. He hit the wipers, sending the little bastard fluttering down Plume Street as he rolled with traffic.

Ballentine took him through the slums and industrial parks south of downtown until it speared the Beach Boulevard. He kept on straight toward the river. Two blocks down, a welder's torch beaconed in the hazy blue sky above a chain-link fence. A minute later he levered into park at the cinderblock headquarters of AAAction Auto Parts and Metals.

"How you doing this afternoon?" Harry tried the friendly angle.

The deskman gave Harry the once-over. "Hot as hell is how I'm doing." A fan blew the guy's cigar smoke out the crank-opened casements.

"Yeah. Warm one, all right." Nothing. "Look, I need a front-end part for a '50 Hudson Commodore."

"Shit, what kinda part? There's lots of different ones."

"Steering. You got any?"

Spit. "Might still be one of them heaps over by the far fence in the corner of the yard. You can go over and look. Strip the part you want and bring it back in. I'll figure the charge. Got a wrench?"

"No, I—"

Bang. The guy tossed a crescent on the counter. "Buck an hour rental. Plus a buck for security. Money up front." In a tattered poster taped on the back wall, a topless gal in a Texaco hat beamed and handled a pump nozzle.

Harry slipped over a deuce and took the wrench. "Say over in the corner? Any landmark or anything so I can find it?"

"Shit, you're the one who knows Hudsons." The guy snickered. "If we still got it, it's a maroon one. Stacked in with the rest of them busted-down heaps back there."

"Thanks."

"Watch out for snakes."

Harry raised a hand against the hard afternoon light. The gravel path gave way to baked mud rills weaving through stacks of junked cars. He picked his way in the general direction of the guy's thumb thrust back. The clay gave way to tufts of grass burned the color of copperheads. Harry picked up a length of trim chrome and kept moving, swishing the grass for snakes while mopping his brow. He stopped in the shade made by a sandwich of three surplused navy jeeps and lit a cigarette. The fence was a line over. He tossed the trim and headed that way.

The cars weren't antiques like he'd expected. Hell, most of them were just a couple years gone. Still had some go in them. Junked anyway. Headlights staring out like passed-over pups at the pound.

A line up, a Mercury like his collapsed on four steel rims. Eaten by rust from the inside out.

Harry kept going until the trail ended at the chain-link fence. Black Nash, aqua Pontiac, then something wine red. He stepped over and rapped on the sun-bleached fender of a once-maroon Hudson. A '49 by the tail lights. Close enough. He stepped around to the heavy grille and popped the hood. Engine gone. He pushed away the nest of rusted cables and wires and danced the wrench down the steering column until it rang against a tangle of levers and widgets jointed to the tie rods. Bingo.

Harry loosened his tie and got to work. A few curses and bloody knuckles later, he surfaced with a sweat-soaked shirt and a rusted connecting arm. He looked it over and felt the heft. *This'll do*, Harry thought. He dropped the Hudson's hood and headed back to pay the man.

"No messages, Harry. Not—look, George says he needs to talk to you. Hold on." *Buzz*

"Harry Boy! Hey, what's that bell?"

"Oh. I'm at a gas station on Colley. Interviewing the mechanic. Somebody's filling a tire." Harry cupped the receiver away from the pinball machine clanging away in the corner.

George grinned as he leaned back under the Sigma Pi rush paddle he'd mounted on his office wall. Virginia '47. "Glad I caught you, old man. A mess here, I'm afraid. Adams came back early and is on an awful tear."

"I thought he was scheduled for court."

"Was. Seems Junior effed-up a redirect so badly that Judge Hitchens adjourned early." George laughed. "Adams has the poor little bastard in his office right now."

"No wonder the old man's pissed."

"I'm afraid it's not just that, old boy. We got a notice letter from Mitcher over at Tickmann and Leach. Seems that they're taking one of your car cases. The one over in Windsor."

"Shit."

"Yep. Sounds like your client wasn't happy with the pace of things."

"I'll call him."

"No use, old man. He's already signed with Mitch."

"What did Adams say?"

"'I'll barbecue his ass' is what I believe he mentioned. That's why I wanted to warn you off, Harry Boy. I'd stay out this afternoon. Tomorrow, too, if you can swing it." George doodled the shuttered windows of a two-story Georgian on a legal pad. "He said you have until next week to show a draft motion and plan."

"What? Next week?"

"Precisely."

"Damn. Wait. Okay, I'll have something. Tell him I've got a solid basis to proceed. No, an actual defective part like the ones that caused the accidents, being reviewed by an expert right now."

"Really."

"Really. Tell him I'll have it in the office day after tomorrow."

George inked a heavy question mark above his little dream house. "Well, see you then, old man. Cheers!" *Click.*

"Jackass." Harry cradled the pay phone receiver and headed back to his booth at Tommy Ming's Chop Suey and Beer Palace on Diamond Springs Road. He siphoned the last two inches of Schlitz and periscoped a finger for a refill. The cast-iron connecting arm sat on a paper mat decorated with prints of palm trees and hula girls. He'd wiped down the rusted metal with a beer-dipped napkin. The thing was just a rusted lump of metal. *Hell, it could've come off a washing machine*, Harry conceded to himself. And it didn't look too defective. *Maybe work on the little slots and grooves with a chisel?* He sat back against the padded vinyl. *And who the hell is going to expertly testify that the freshly chipped thing caused a wreck? That dope Chauncey over at Pep Boys?* Tommy's wife slid the new bottle over and went back to washing glasses.

Some brainstorm.

The first rule of procedure, Harry had figured out in

eleven years of legal practice, is that you can freely
bullshit most anybody but don't try it on yourself. He was
out of bullshit, anyway. He stuck the little control arm
into his jacket pocket and retreated to the fresh beer.

Two hours later, Harry stepped out in the gravel lot
carrying his jacket and a paper bag. Ming had sold him six
to go. Harry fired a Carlton and tossed the match. The
day's heat rose from the hard-packed dirt. The Merc
slouched over in the corner beneath a neon palm. Night
was near and that backseat looked like his best bet.
Couple more, sleep it off. Maybe go back inside for an
early breakfast. But when he got to the car, Harry climbed
in the driver's and jangled the keys. He felt like driving.

Diamond Springs ran north to the bay. Strung along
the way were a few boatyards and bait shops, a filling
station now and then—last chances before the ferry over
to Cape Charles. Harry rode with the top down and a
cool can between his legs. He caught a red light. In the
field across the way, a couple of kids launched bottle
rockets behind a fireworks stand. The little missiles
sizzled up fifty feet and banged in a quick shower of
sparks. When the light went green, he kept rolling to
nowhere in particular.

Up ahead the north sky cooled to indigo. The radio
played Miles Davis' "Out of the Blue." Harry drove
another mile, past a finger of pine woods, and caught the
smell of salt. He followed it to Shore Drive, hooking a
way-wide left and riding up the curb. Harry steadied back

on the dashed white line and steered with his fingertips, a trick he'd picked up listening to cops waiting to testify in traffic court. Marinas and piers of the Amphib Base passed by on the right, freshwater lakes on the left—a hydrologic quirk that for some reason taunted him each time he drove through here. He'd get a map and figure it out sometime. He cleared a bridge and flipped on the headlights just as a rise of sand and live oaks signaled the end of East Ocean View.

Harry turned into the beat-down East Beach settlement of shotgun one-stories, by-the-week motels, and a couple of working streetlights. He'd been back in here once before for some reason he couldn't place. A sign indicated his location—25th Bay and Pleasant. A block up, the ragged tar and concrete t-boned a sand path paralleling the shore dunes. He stayed on the gas and sailed through, slewing and plowing sand for maybe fifty feet until the Mercury was axle-deep and out of luck.

Harry killed the motor. A few houses sheltered behind the dunes flanking the car. Lights shone in one. It was dead quiet except for an occasional roller coming up on the beach. He rustled the paper bag for a fresh beer and lit a cigarette before climbing out onto the sand. He looked around. There stretched the open bay, luminous against the sky.

An owl called from the black trees.

Harry plopped against the fender and pulled off his shoes, tossing them over the windshield onto the front seat. He rolled up his trousers for the walk down to the beach. He left the keys dangling in the ignition.

The path wound through patches of sea grass and

sunburned briar, up the sand slope, and down through a wind-blown parapet to the empty beach. Harry slogged through the soft sand to a bowl in the dune face. He surrendered and sat.

"Ouch."

Harry pulled the forgotten control arm from his pocket. He studied the thing for a last, hopeful moment before tossing it behind a nearby dune. *What the hell now?* He leaned back, head against sand that had gone cool in the evening air.

Harry opened his eyes and scanned the bay, now gone a dull blue. No ship lights out in the Atlantic channel. Odd. The stars twinkled on one by one across the northern sky. He recognized the Big Dipper. The rest were always a mystery.

The swell pushed up to the tide line and slipped back into the sea.

Light danced on the receding wash. Harry followed it up to a bright light pacing across the velvet sky, maybe a mile down the beach. He propped on an elbow and squinted a hard look. Just a plane coming into the airport.

Harry pushed himself up, got another cigarette going and walked down to the water. A lip of tide washed across his feet. The wet sand stiffened as he kept going, wading up to his knees in the warm water. His feet found a bar running out toward the breakwater, so he followed it until he was waist deep, the water like warm ink around him. He considered diving in and swimming out to the black rocks. *Yeah, hell, why not?* He got a good last pull on the nub, the tip glowing hot tangerine before he flicked it, hissing, into the bay. The approaching airliner caught his eye again as a second wing light flashed on. A breeze came from the west, carrying the engine noise away from him. The glowing blue-white landing lights now appeared to hover out over the bay. *A trick of geometry and nighttime distance,* Harry estimated as he took another step.

A sound came up the beach. *Maybe a door closing,* Harry guessed, looking back to the line of dunes. He turned back to the water, just as the plane's lights blued and intensified. Harry waited for the engine roar, but the lights split into two groups that began to silently move apart.

"Now what the—?" Harry crab-stepped back onto the sandbar and watched. In a second, the left group of lights flared rust-orange and rocketed straight out toward the Atlantic. The other lights seem to come closer, then flicked out.

Harry sloshed back to the beach, almost falling, searching for any sign of the plane. *Maybe it was a jet interceptor or a missile of some kind.* At the touch of dry sand, he stopped and listened for a rumble or boom.

"Well, damn, that..."

The dimpled sand flared pure white and sharp shadows as a new light flashed above the beach. Harry shielded his eyes and watched the damn thing flicker and dim before gliding out to sea. It disappeared a minute later.

Harry fumbled in his shirt pocket, fishing out a cigarette. The match flared orange and hissed out as he tossed it in the wet sand. He scanned the sky. Only the stars flickered away now. Harry smoked the stick down to the filter, ventured a last look out over the black water, then headed for the dunes.

Just what in the hell had happened?

Harry found a man who helped him push the car out of the sand. Harry gave the guy the last cans of beer and headed for home.

Two days later the dodo bird bobbed away under the desk light that Harry hadn't turned off, the pivots making an almost inaudible, rhythmic squeak on the tin legs. The slat of sunlight had burned way past the clock and given way to the orange glow of streetlamps. An office note with *Harry, please see me* was taped over by another with *Harry, where are you?* written in Buck Adams's heavy block script.

Harry sat on the edge of the dune, cigarette going, watching the night sky. Waves curled in and combed the beach. He held the tip near the watch face. Almost nine. Just stars and a few southbound planes miles overhead slowly working their way down the coast. A ship moved across the limb of the bay, heading to sea.

"They ain't coming tonight, I don't think."

Harry turned to see an old woman standing on the far side of the path. A window was illuminated in the cottage behind her.

"How's that?"

The woman shuffled over. She wore a flannel bed coat.

"Them lights." She watched him. "Got a cigarette?"

Harry passed her the pack and cupped a match.

"You saw them?"

"Thanks, hon." She took a good drag. "Oh, yeah. Seen 'em all week. Damn things flying around, snapping off like flashbulbs." She blew a steam of smoke down the beach. "Seen you out here watching 'em night before last," she said, smiling a little.

"Probably just planes."

"You hopin' they'd be back tonight, huh?"

Harry stared back out at the water.

"Me, too," she said, cackling on another drag of smoke. "Don't look like they're coming, though. Too windy I'm guessing."

"How's that?" Harry didn't get the connection.

She chuckled. "The other night. The bay was smooth enough for the Sweet Lord Jesus to walk to Baltimore. Been like that all week. They only come when it's like that."

Harry smiled and figured she was drunk or plain nuts. "Well, likely they were just some reflections, then."

The woman scanned the horizon. "You know, them things don't appear for just anybody." She locked on Harry's eyes as she pulled on the cigarette and waved down the line of houses facing the beach. "Neighbors swear they ain't seen a thing. They all think I'm crazy," she said, giving a little chuckle. "Oh, meant to give you this." She rustled something from her coat pocket.

Harry hefted the paper sack.

"Saw you toss it in the sand the other night. Figured you might need it."

"Oh. Yeah, thanks." A little embarrassed, Harry stuffed the useless little arm in his jacket. He turned back to the bay.

"Listen," she said, stepping closer. "I ain't crazy. These things here the two of us seen, they're signs and prophets. And they ain't done is what I think. That's why you come back this evening. You're part of the matter."

Harry turned to say something but the old woman was watching the sky.

"Harry, a Mr. Baxter on line two." Paula's voice buzzed from the speaker beside the telephone.

"Harry?"

Click.

"Harry, are you there?"

The ceiling fan spun above the darkened office. The little bird squeaked and sipped at the glass of water. Up and down. Right next to a paper sack and a steering connecting arm from a 1949 Hudson, silvery new and showing a hairline crack along the tie bushing where the casting appeared defective.

Good luck, honey, read the note.

Harry Bynde sat at his desk, toying a magnifying glass in the shaft of light escaping the blinds, making circles shimmer and dance on the far wall.

IN THE TRENCHES

By R. G. Koepf

MONDAY

Not morning already. Sarah groaned to herself as she rolled over. *It's too early to get up.*

Although she had room-darkening shades, her bedroom windows faced south, and she could see glimmers of daylight through the draperies at sunrise. She opened one eye, but it was still dark outside.

I don't want to get up yet, she argued with her body. Sarah rolled over to snuggle up against her husband, and then remembered that he was out of town for a few days.

After a few minutes, however, her mind won, and she reluctantly crawled out of bed.

A glance at the clock confirmed that it was really too early to get up. *Five o'clock! Good grief!*

When Sarah was younger and had her children to care for, she didn't mind waking up early so she could have a few minutes to herself before the morning chaos.

Now that they were grown and out of the house, however, she liked to sleep in, just a little, just once in a while. Most mornings, she didn't have that luxury. Although she only worked part-time several days a week, she liked to keep to a regular schedule and tried to get up at the same time every morning. In the summer months, an early wake-up call meant she could enjoy the sunrise over the beach, alone with the waves and the gulls. In the winter, like this morning, she didn't like to go outside in the dark and the cold. Her doctor warned her about tripping and falling in the dark. He didn't want to see her for any broken bones. Since there was still a lot of construction going on in the neighborhood, she didn't want to take any chances in the winter darkness.

The construction seemed never-ending. This day was no different. As she drove home from work that afternoon, she saw that a large trench had been dug across the street, right in front of her house on Chesapeake Drive. *Now what?* she asked herself as she pulled into the garage. A new house was being built across the street. The hole in the street was probably due to that construction. After she parked the car in the garage, Sarah walked over to the trench and looked down. The hole looked at least ten feet deep, maybe more.

Sarah forgot to mention the trench to her husband, Scott, when he called that evening from his business trip. *It will probably be filled in by the weekend when he gets back,* she thought as she hung up the phone. *I won't bother him with it.*

TUESDAY

What's today? Oh, yes, Tuesday. I have a staff meeting.
Sarah was a financial advisor for a large insurance firm.
She had worked hard over the years to reach that
position, and enjoyed her job of helping people achieve
their life goals. She and her husband had been fortunate
early in his career, and their investing strategies had been
fruitful. That's why they could afford to live in their
dream home by the Chesapeake Bay. After years of living
in rentals and cheaply built houses around the country,
they'd designed and built a custom home in a new
neighborhood in Norfolk, Virginia.

Life in East Beach was good. On the mornings Sarah
didn't have to rush to the office for an early morning
meeting, she would dress in her workout clothes and go
to the neighborhood gym, ride her bike, or just jog on the
beach, depending on the weather. She varied her activities
and enjoyed seeing neighbors and the natural beauty of
the bay.

This particular morning, since she was up earlier than
usual, Sarah decided to read before it was time to go to
the office. *I'll take a cup of coffee up to the cupola,* she thought.
Darn! I forgot I'm out of coffee, she moaned. She hated to
admit it, but she was addicted to that morning hot brew
of caffeine. She had only three daily doses, one at home
and two more at the office, and that normally sufficed.
There had been persistent rumors of a Starbucks coffee
shop to be built nearby, and finally construction had
started. It was agonizingly slow, however, and until it was

open, the only place close by to get coffee at this early hour was the nearby 7-11 convenience store.

Sarah considered that option, but this morning decided against going to the store, coming home, and then going back out to her office. Rather than go up to their third floor cupola to read without coffee, she instead wrote a short letter to her elderly aunt who lived in Wisconsin.

I'll just go to the office a little early and make coffee there, she decided.

Later, as she backed out of the garage into the narrow alley, Sarah wished she had gotten that cup of hot java. Still coffee-deprived, she suddenly heard the backing alarm on her car. Sarah slammed on the brakes. *That's odd,* she thought. *There shouldn't be anything there.* Her car was an older model and didn't have the fancy back-up camera that newer models had, so she had to get out in the cold and look. In the early morning light, she could see what set off the backing alarm: an orange construction barrel warning motorists and pedestrians about the long trench in the street. She had forgotten all about it. "Close call," she said, then sighed.

As she got back in her car to drive out of the neighborhood, Sarah had to slam on her brakes again. An animal darted across the road in front of her, running away from the trench. *Was it a fox? Or a dog?* Although there was a citywide leash law, some neighbors allowed their dogs to run off-leash. Sarah didn't see any one around, so assumed it was a fox. Although construction had disturbed their habitat, wild foxes still lived in the sand dunes beside the bay. She occasionally saw the animals on her sunrise walks on the beach. She was wary of them, as there had been reports of rabid foxes in the Hampton Roads region.

After the close encounter with the animal, Sarah drove more cautiously, avoiding other orange construction barrels and excavations in the road. She sighed again. She had hoped that by now, after five years, construction in the neighborhood would be finished. Sarah and Scott had searched the East Coast shoreline for potential retirement locations, and were thrilled when they heard about East Beach. "A quaint seaside village," read the brochure. Driving through the barely built neighborhood for the first time, that's exactly what Sarah and Scott envisioned. They stopped in the sales office, and after a tour of the fledging development with the sales manager, they signed a lot contract that day. They didn't want to live in a "new construction" neighborhood again, but the call of the sea was too strong, and they agreed to do it one last time.

WEDNESDAY

The next morning, a strange noise startled Sarah from her sleep. *What was that?* she wondered. She glanced at the clock. *Three o'clock in the morning. Good Grief!!*

Annoyed, Sarah tried to go back to sleep. Houses were still being built close all around her house, and it seemed the noises never ceased. She had grown accustomed to the usual suspects—the roar of commercial and military airplanes overhead, the rumble of garbage trucks and lumber delivery trucks, the yapping of neighbors' dogs—but this morning, really in the dead of night, the sound was different. Loud enough to awaken her, but then silent. Sarah listened intently, but all she heard was the crashing of the waves on the beach below her house.

Sarah rolled over. This morning was her day off from work, and she had hoped to sleep late. She didn't have any other commitments or appointments. No quilt guild, no book club, no bridge club. East Beach was a very social neighborhood, and there was never a lack of activities. Today was unusual in that she had nothing planned.

Sarah was wide awake now, wondering about the noise. She struggled to recall what it sounded like. It was a muffled sound, almost like voices, but not really voices. She thought she'd also heard scraping, like something metal. It sounded like, well, she really couldn't place it. She finally drifted back to sleep to the soothing sounds of the waves.

She slept soundly until another muffled noise awakened her. *I didn't set the alarm,* she thought. *What is that? It almost sounds like a ring tone.* She checked her alarm clock, just to make sure it wasn't her clock. It wasn't. The ringing stopped.

Later that morning, as she was enjoying her second cup of coffee up in her cupola, Sarah enjoyed the view of the neighborhood. Construction on the house across the street seemed to be rather slow. Sarah and Scott had not yet met the new neighbors, although they had seen them at the house once or twice. Sarah spotted the woman she thought might be the owner, walking around the unfinished house. *Maybe I'll ask her over for coffee*, Sarah thought to herself.

Sarah finished her drink, and as she descended the spiral stairs and then downstairs to the main floor, she thought she heard the ringing noise again. After grabbing her warm jacket, she walked carefully across the street to the new house, avoiding the trench. A neighbor was walking her dog, tugging on the leash, trying to keep her pet from going too near the gaping hole. Something seemed to be attracting the animal.

The new neighbor was nowhere in sight, although several cars were parked out front. Sarah knocked on the temporary builder's door. She could hear the *kchew-kchew-kchew* of a nail gun. She knocked louder. Finally, the woman she had seen earlier slowly opened the door. "Yes, may I help you?" she asked Sarah.

"Hi! I'm Sarah. I live across the street. Are you the new owner? I thought you might like to come over for a cup of coffee."

The woman opened the door wider. "It's very nice to meet you, Sarah. I'm Becky. I'd love to get out of this cold house and join you for a hot cup of coffee, but I'm waiting for Ralph Finkelstine, my architect. We had an appointment at ten, but he hasn't shown up yet. Would you be free for lunch?"

"Sure, that would be great. I'll come back over at noon. We can go to the Sandfiddler Café, right across from the neighborhood. I'm happy to drive."

Becky smiled. "I'd like that."

Sarah also smiled and turned to go back home. She

faced Becky and said, "Ralph is notorious for being late. I've heard from some of the neighbors whose houses he has designed that they often have to reschedule appointments because he is late or a no-show. I hope he shows."

"Me, too," Becky said as Sarah walked away.

Sarah enjoyed some light reading while waiting for her lunch date. She really wanted to sit down at her sewing machine and work on her latest quilt, but didn't want to start sewing and then have to stop after a short time.

As she sat reading, and occasionally looking at the whitecaps on the bay, she thought she heard the ringing noise again. "Maybe I need my ears checked," she said to herself, then laughed.

She tried to read, but was distracted. Besides sewing, she also thought about her latest writing project that she planned to work on in the afternoon. Although the book she was reading was a mystery by one of her favorite authors, Jayne Ormerod, Sarah had trouble focusing on the story. Her mind kept wandering back to the strange noises that had awakened her that morning, and wondered about Becky, her new neighbor. She was glad they would be having lunch together.

Sarah knew most of the neighbors who, like her, had moved to East Beach within the past few years. She made it a point to meet her immediate neighbors, and met new neighbors at one of the many neighborhood social events such as First Friday and the monthly wine nights. Others she met during her walks on the beach or around the neighborhood. Many of the neighbors were known by their dogs.

Sarah's stomach grumbled, and told her it was almost lunchtime. She looked forward to her upcoming date with her new neighbor. The café was close enough to walk to when the weather was nice, but today was windy and cold, so Sarah would drive them. After brushing her hair and freshening up her make-up, Sarah backed her car out of the garage and into the alley. This time, she was careful to watch out for the trench in the street. *I wonder how long before they fill it in?* she groused to herself.

She carefully maneuvered her car around the trench and parked in front of Becky's house. Before she could open her door, Becky came out and got in the car.

"You're prompt," Becky said. "Are you as hungry as I am? Being in the cold house without heat has made me hungry."

"Yes, I'm hungry, too. I think you'll like the Sandfiddler. It's one of our favorite places."

The drive to the café was so short that the ladies only had a few minutes to chat.

"Did Ralph show up?" Sarah asked.

"No, he never did. I called his cell phone but it went straight to voice mail. So I called the office but the receptionist said she hadn't seen him all morning. He had appointments and she didn't expect him in the office until this afternoon."

"Oh." Sarah paused, wondering whether to say more to her new neighbor. "He's often late. He doesn't bother to call to let people know, either. Quite rude, in my opinion."

"Hopefully, I'll hear from him and we can reschedule. Since my husband is still traveling for his new job, it falls on me to get things done for the house."

"Where do you live now?"

"We're moving from DC. We both wanted to get out of the rat race up there."

Sarah understood. Years before, she and Scott had made the same decision.

The Sandfiddler Café was busy, but they were seated promptly at a booth along a side wall.

"Lunch is on me," Sarah told Becky.

"Thanks. I'll treat next time." Becky glanced around the bustling restaurant. "This place is so cute. I like all the beachy décor."

Sarah agreed. "It is cute. The items on the wall—"

Sarah stopped speaking when the waitress appeared. The young woman took their drink orders and said she'd give them a few minutes before taking their food orders.

Since it was Becky's first visit, Sarah explained the menu. "There are daily specials, and everything on the menu is good. Even though it's lunchtime, you can have breakfast if you want. Their eggs benedict and pancakes are the best. For lunch, my husband and I like the Reuben. The fries are great, too."

"How long have you lived here?" Becky asked as she glanced at the laminated menu.

"About five years. We moved from DC, too."

"Do you work? I'm still looking for a job. We relocated based on Tim's promotion."

"Yes, but just part-time. At this stage in my life, I have too many other interests to work full-time. My husband took an early retirement from the defense contractor he worked for, and now has his own consulting business. He is traveling this week, but he doesn't have to go out of town too often."

"Must be nice," said the younger woman.

"Yes, it is." Sarah smiled.

The sound of the "Happy Birthday" song drew their attention to a nearby table. The waitresses had gathered around an embarrassed customer, and one of them set a cupcake with a candle in front of her. After the song, their waitress returned to their table and took their orders.

"Not to be nosy," Sarah said after the waitress left, "but what was your meeting with Ralph about? Some neighbors and builders have found him to be quite peculiar about arbitrary details. I've heard from several sources that he has had heated arguments with various people who work for the city."

Becky paused before answering. "After construction started, we realized we wanted to make a few changes to the kitchen area, which involves moving a window. The builder said we had to submit the architect's revised plans to the Design Committee, and Ralph said he wanted to look at the house again before he redrew the plans for us to submit to the Design Committee."

"I'm sure he'll show up or call. Change of subject. So what kind of job are you looking for? Maybe I can help."

"I'm a registered Realtor, but I'd really like to do something different. I know it's a tough sales market right now. I've always thought about writing, but have never done anything with that thought."

"We have a great Writers' Guild! Our next meeting is this Friday morning. We'd love to have you join us. One of our members has just published his latest book, *Threshold*, and he is talking about developing characters. We meet in the clubhouse library at nine, and are usually finished by eleven. Please come!"

"Are you sure? I'm not yet a real writer. It's just something I've thought about."

"That's not a problem. We have all levels of experience. I'm not published yet, although I have written some short stories and newspaper articles."

"Then I'd love to come."

"Great!"

Just then the waitress brought their lunch orders. "This looks good," Becky said.

"I hope you like it," Sarah replied. The two ladies enjoyed their lunches and their conversation, talking about their families, their houses and the region.

A young woman approached their table. "May I help you?" Sarah asked.

"Oh, excuse me. I just wanted to take a closer look at that ceramic mermaid," the woman said.

"Oh, sure," Sarah told her.

After the woman walked away, Becky said, "That was odd."

Sarah explained about the woman's behavior. "The original owner knew local crafts people and convinced them to display their artwork to help with decorating the new restaurant. She didn't charge them a commission, so they essentially had a free gallery. Most of the pieces are for sale. It's fun to see new things as artwork sells. It's a little unnerving, though, like just now, when strangers come up to your table while you're eating because they want to take a closer look at the artwork or check the price."

On the short trip back into the neighborhood, Sarah made a comment about the construction. "I will be so glad when all of this is finished. I almost backed into the trench in our street."

"I know what you mean. Why did they dig up the street?"

"Not sure. Happens a lot. I thought it had something to do with your construction."

"Not sure why that would be."

Sarah stopped the car in front of her new neighbor's house. "Hope you hear from Ralph," she said.

"Me, too."

They exchanged contact information and agreed to meet at the Writers' Guild meeting in two days, if not before.

Sarah parked her car in the garage and smiled as she entered her home. *What a nice, new neighbor we have,* she thought. *We'll have to invite them over for dinner.*

Sarah spent the afternoon as she had planned, sewing in her studio on the second floor. Although sometimes the spectacular views of the Chesapeake Bay were distracting, she usually found the sea inspired her. This day, the bay did not disappoint. A strong northerly wind sent the waves crashing on the breakers. Sarah was invigorated by the view almost as much as by taking a walk on the beach.

THURSDAY

The next morning, Sarah almost drove into the gaping trench in the street again. Beyond annoyed, she was angry. There was no excuse for the huge hole to remain in the middle of the street.

She stopped her car, got out, and glared down into the trench with her hands on her hips. Was it her imagination, or was there more dirt in the hole than the other day? Why didn't they fill it in all the way?

A neighbor walking her dog passed by. "Hi, Sarah. Come on, Duke, that's not for you." The dog seemed interested in the hole and was sniffing all around the edges.

When she reached her office, she placed a call to the city inspector's office, hoping to talk to the City Code Inspector, Jake Stone.

"Good morning. This is Sarah Smith, an East Beach resident. I'd like to speak to Jake Stone."

The receptionist, who seemed barely awake, replied, "I'm sorry, Mr. Stone isn't in."

"When do you expect him?"

"He usually comes in by ten."

"May I leave a message for him to call me?"

"I guess."

"Please tell him that Mrs. Smith would like to speak

with him about the trench on Chesapeake Drive."

"How do you spell that?"

Geesh, Sarah thought, *who hired her?*

Sarah waited all day for a return phone call from Jake. She never heard from him. *Who's minding the store?* she wondered. She worked late that day, and city offices were closed by the time she returned home. *I'll call again tomorrow,* she told herself.

That evening, Sarah phoned her new neighbor Becky.

"Hi, it's Sarah. I'm calling to see if you can still attend the Writers' Guild meeting tomorrow morning."

"Thanks for the reminder. Yes! I'd love to meet some other neighbors and see if this group is for me."

"Great! If you come to my house, we can walk to the clubhouse together. Our meetings start promptly at nine, so if you want to come to my house a few minutes early, that would be fine."

"Sure. See you tomorrow."

"Oh, by the way, did Ralph ever show up?"

"No, and I've left several voice mail messages for him."

"Hmm, that's strange. Well, you should hear from him soon. See you tomorrow. Bye."

"Bye."

FRIDAY

The next morning dawned bright and sunny, but the north wind was howling. Sarah climbed to the cupola to watch the whitecaps on the bay. Her house was well built, and even though winter was shrieking outside, she felt snug and secure. It hadn't been easy to build the house, especially with all the design changes they'd had to make, but once it was finished and they had moved in, the pain and anguish of constructing their own dream house was behind them. Forgotten just like labor and delivery of a baby was forgotten by a woman as soon as she held her baby in her arms.

Sarah looked forward to the monthly Writers' Guild meetings. Most of the members were neighbors, but there was a special bond between the members that went beyond living in the same neighborhood. They were all very supportive of each other's efforts as writers. Sarah genuinely liked each of them.

Becky arrived at her door promptly at 8:45. "Good morning." Sarah welcomed her inside. "Come in out of the wind for a few minutes."

"Brrr, it is downright chilly this morning! Do you think it will snow?"

"Not today." Sarah laughed. "Although we have had big snowfalls in past years. The air is too dry. Just the north wind today."

A few minutes later, the ladies bundled up warmly for the short walk to the clubhouse. The wind was so fierce that they didn't chat on the way.

Once inside, however, the room was warm and abuzz with conversation. Many members had arrived early, to refill their coffee mugs and catch up with each other.

Sarah interrupted the chatter. "Hi, everyone! I'd like

you to meet our newest neighbor and member. This is Becky, who is building across the street from me."

"Welcome. Hi, I'm Anne, the Guild President. We're so glad you came."

Other members introduced themselves in turn, and Becky's face flushed as they bombarded her with questions.

"Where are you moving from?"

"Have you published anything?"

"Who's your builder?"

Sarah finally saved her new friend. "Whoa! She'll tell all in her new book which is coming out next month."

The group chuckled in unison.

As members topped off their coffee mugs and began to sit, Sarah overheard Clark and Anne talking.

"I've been waiting all week and he hasn't called back," Anne said. "I really need to get approval so we can move forward on our spring landscaping."

"I had a call in, too, but he seems to be AWOL."

"Who are you talking about?" Sarah asked, although she already had her suspicions.

"Ralph Finkelstine," Anne said. "He said he could recommend a landscaper for us. We're anxious to hire one. They get so busy that you have to start in the winter time."

Clark chimed in. "He hasn't called me, either. I can't move forward with my mortgage package until I get his final plans," he said.

Anne called the meeting to order and welcomed Becky. "We're so glad you could join us. We start every meeting with updates on our projects. Would you like to share?"

Becky was a little flustered. "I haven't even written my first novel. I just thought I would like to write, and Sarah invited me today. I feel like such a newbie."

"Not to worry," Anne reassured her. "We all started out like you, and in fact, we have several members who are fledging writers. This group is for everyone."

After the meeting, Sarah lingered. She wanted to talk to Anne and Clark some more about the missing Ralph Finkelstine and Jake Stone. Becky was talking to some of the other members.

Sarah inserted herself into the conversation between Anne and Clark. "So you haven't heard from Ralph all week? Becky had a meeting with him the other morning, but he never showed. I've been trying to call Jake about the trench in the street, and he seems to be AWOL, too."

The monthly wine social was that evening, at the clubhouse. Sarah invited Becky, but she had other plans. Sarah and Scott usually attended, but rarely stayed late. They enjoyed visiting with their neighbors, especially during the cold season, because they saw fewer people outside around the neighborhood. In warm weather, people walked the streets and enjoyed the sea breezes on their porches.

With Scott out of town until tomorrow, Sarah went

by herself. Conversation that evening was lively and included theories about the missing architect and city inspector. They both had missed several appointments with residents, and others had been waiting for return phone calls.

Sarah was more concerned about the open trench in front of her house, however. She wasn't the only one. Another neighbor who lived on the same street asked, "Did anyone notice the trench on Chesapeake Drive? My dog and others can't seem to keep away from it."

Sarah chimed in, "I tried to call the City Inspector about getting it filled in, but Jake Stone seems to be AWOL. No one else is doing anything about it."

"Ralph's car is still parked at the sales office, but no one has seen him for a few days."

Another neighbor added her opinion. "I heard he was having marital and financial troubles."

"Hey, did you see the guy on the pink Vespa the other day? Awfully cold to be riding a scooter. Seems like more of a warm weather ride. I don't know who it was, but I saw him talking to Jake in his city truck the other day as I was walking Duke. When they saw me walking by and looking at them, they stopped talking. Their conversation looked rather heated."

The small talk finally drifted onto other matters, and the wine flowed. Sarah finally called it an evening. "Scott gets home tomorrow," she told her friends, "so I need a good night's sleep."

Sarah set her alarm for the next morning, so she wouldn't be late picking up her husband from the airport. She was glad he was coming home tomorrow.

But Sarah had a hard time falling asleep. There was a reason that she enjoyed mystery stories. She had a curious mind, and enjoyed solving puzzles. The events of the past week tumbled over and over in her mind. Where was Ralph Finkelstine? Where was Jake Stone? What was the purpose of the trench? What was that strange noise she'd heard? What was the ringing she kept hearing?

SATURDAY

Bzzzzzz! Bzzzzzz! The alarm buzzer was loud. Sarah hit the snooze bar and then realized she didn't have more time to sleep. *Scott's coming home today!* She smiled. She had missed him this week, especially with all the strange happenings.

Since Scott had retired from full-time work, the couple spent most of their time together except when Sarah was at her office or Scott was traveling. Scott kept telling her she could stop working, but she wasn't quite ready to give up her career.

Before she left the house, Sarah confirmed that Scott's plane was due to arrive on time. She was glad. In the winter, flights were often delayed due to storms.

As they waited for Scott's suitcase at the baggage carousel, Sarah started to tell Scott about the week's events. An engineer by education and experience, her husband was the more logical one in the relationship. He always had an explanation for strange happenings. This time, however, even he was at a loss for rational explanations.

Sarah loved Scott for his sense of humor, but this time he was being ridiculous. "Maybe they took off together to a deserted island," he joked as they loaded his bag in the car for the short ride home. "Maybe they both decided they wanted to leave their wives."

"I think Jake is single," Sarah said, "and I don't think Ralph could afford to leave his wife. Even though he has designed a lot of houses, I don't think he makes much money. His wife is a bank VP and makes oodles of money."

"How do you know?" Scott asked.

"Oh, just neighborhood talk. I don't repeat gossip, but so many people have mentioned it that it must be true."

"Well, it does seem strange," Scott agreed with her. "But I'm sure there is a reason for their absences this week. Maybe they both had illnesses or deaths in their families. So how was the rest of your week, honey?"

"I kept hearing strange noises," Sarah confided. "I think I may need to see the doctor. For several days, I kept hearing a ringing in my ears. But I haven't heard any more since yesterday."

"I'm sure you're fine," Scott reassured her. "Probably just the wind and being alone in the house. You said the north wind howled all week."

"Yes, that's probably all it was. But what about the noises in the middle of the night? I know I didn't imagine that!"

"You know there are stray cats and foxes around. It was probably just an animal fight."

"It didn't sound like animals, but you're probably right. You always are. Just be careful driving. There is a huge trench in the road in front of our house."

"What's the trench for?"

"I don't know," Sarah replied as they headed for East Beach. "But I almost drove into it several times. It's been partially filled in, but not all the way. I'm just glad you're back."

"Me, too," Scott said. "What's for supper?"

EPILOGUE

Two days later, Ralph and Jake were still missing. Ralph's wife had called the police and an intensive search was conducted. Despite the best efforts of local police, there were no clues regarding the sudden disappearance of either man.

The trench remained a gaping hole on Chesapeake Drive until a neighborhood dog fell in and began pawing furiously at the dirt. His owner called 9-1-1 for help to retrieve his dog. By the time the fire department arrived, a group of neighbors had surrounded the hole and were all staring down into the trench.

As the firemen fought through the crowd and walked up to the hole, they saw what the neighbors were watching. The dog was tugging on a shirt, tattered and dirty, and partially covering a bloody arm.

ZINNIAS ALWAYS BLOOM

By Mary-Jac O'Daniel

For military spouses, one question often arises when you tell a new acquaintance how many times you have moved. *Which move was the hardest?* For me, it is a complicated question, because though the time was dark and trying, the memory fills me with warmth. Instead of darkness, when I think back to that period of my life, a patchwork of faces and colors fill my head. Among those images, the most vibrant are the red-haired child, Makenna, and zinnias.

We moved that fall to the seaside community of East Beach, a quiet area in Norfolk, Virginia. A beautiful array of beach houses, many with large wrap-around porches, surrounded us. From the upstairs window, we could see the sea grass blowing in the wind, along with a glimpse of the water, before it melted into the horizon. The house was great, but the word *home*—four simple letters that entailed so much emotion—sounded foreign.

It was a beautiful neighborhood, but I knew no one, and there was no familiarity, which was normally how I defined home. It was just my husband and me, and he had deployed a few weeks earlier. This was the first time I'd moved without his help. The loneliness and stress of the solo move added to the long list of troubles that had welcomed us in the year.

Our household goods arrived a few days earlier. Many of the boxes had been opened and unpacked. However, a few boxes marked "other" still littered the living room floor. I opened one of them. Unaware of the broken shards of glass covering the bottom of the box, I reached in for an item. "Ouch!" I yelled as I ran to the sink and let the water run over my finger, now crimson with blood. It was just a small cut and I grabbed a Band-Aid from our emergency kit. I winced as I secured it tightly around my finger.

Returning to my unpacking, I glanced into the box and saw that the glass had come from a frame that held a photo of my mother and me. In the picture, I was five years old, my tiny hands cradled her chin while I gazed up, my eyes bright with adoration. My mother looked so beautiful in the photo, a stark contrast to this past year, when her beautiful, long blond hair had fallen out after a few rounds of chemo. For four years, she'd fought breast cancer, and six months ago had passed away. I closed my eyes, searching for the perfect memory of her laugh and smile. She had a laugh that belied her delicate features, and new friends were often startled when she would lean her head back and fill the room with her roaring laughter. I wanted to call her, to tell her about the broken frame, moving alone, and ask her how she managed to move alone a few times, with two children. I closed the box, the broken frame another reminder of how broken I felt in the present moment.

The remaining boxes could wait to be unpacked. I made my way to the garage and pulled my hair into a ponytail. I grabbed an old apron I used for gardening from a hook on the garage wall. The words of my mother echoed in my head. "Bloom where you are planted, child," she would say when we made another navy move. Thirteen moves as a child and eight as an adult. That's a lot of tears, many goodbyes, and more lost and broken furniture than I care to count. *You should be used to this by now.* I grabbed the shovel leaning against the garage wall, along with a package of zinnia seeds that had been sitting in the corner, and headed outside.

The smell of the salt from the bay wafted through the air. I carefully dug my small holes and tried to imagine how beautiful the flowers would look when they sprouted.

A little, red-haired girl eyed me curiously from across the street. She leaned against her fence, a jump rope flung over her shoulder. I gave her a cursory smile.

As I turned the soil in preparation for planting, I heard *tap, tap, tap. Whack* went the jump rope as it hit the ground with a thud. The sounds grew closer and closer.

"Watch out!" I snapped at the unsuspecting young girl. "Can't you see I'm planting a garden here?"

I winced as though another piece of glass had just pierced me. Why had I yelled at the child? *It's not you, child, it's me.* I stood up and tried to smile, wiping my dirty hands down the front of my apron.

The child looked at me, at first wide-eyed and confused. She brushed the strands of red hair from her face and I saw her blue eyes filling with tears. Her freckles glistened in the light from the sun and her small fists were clenched at her sides. "I'm s-s-s-sorry," came a low, frightened reply.

The young girl narrowed her eyes, dropped her jump rope, and then kicked her green sneaker into the ground, hard. A cloud of black levitated around me. I tried to duck my head, but the dirt found its way into my hair. I brushed a clump from my scalp, and looked at the small child.

"I hate you. I hate this place," she yelled. Her tears were free-flowing now and she made no effort to stop them.

I wiped the dirt off my clothes and smiled at the young girl. "I just moved here myself. I'm not sure I like it yet, either."

She turned her head away from me and wiped her eyes with the back of her hand. "Sorry about the dirt in your hair. Where did you move from?"

I put the shovel against the fence and walked closer to the young girl. "We just moved from San Diego."

The red-haired girl cast her eyes downward. For a moment, I thought she would cry again. She stared into space, and when she spoke, her voice was barely audible. "We just moved from Hawaii." She glanced at the car in their driveway and pointed at a military sticker. "My daddy's in the Navy." She clenched her fist as she said the words and kicked the dirt around her.

I opened my mouth to make a snide comment about buying me new dirt. I immediately closed it when I looked at her.

Her fists were still clenched, and she blinked hard, as though trying to stop the release of tears again. I remembered my own youth, being settled into a new place and then having to move again. Most moves were okay; I learned how to be resilient, make new friends quickly, to get close, but not too close, knowing I would leave them soon.

My mind drifted back to one move when I'd been in second grade. Recess came, and no one invited me to play. I stood on the periphery of the playground, not daring to ask anyone if I could join their activity. To occupy the time, I began doing gymnastics. Cartwheels, handstands, and walkovers. I lost myself in the movement and forgot that I wasn't alone. Soon I was doing modified versions of tumbling passes I'd learned from my previous gym. I came out of a round-off, and when I lifted my head up, a girl with jet-black hair and golden brown eyes smiled at me.

"Hi," she shyly said. "I'm Linda."

"Hi" I repeated back. "I'm Karen."

She stuck her hand out to me. "I do gymnastics, too."

Soon, we were making up routines together. "Can you do this?" she asked as she did a cartwheel into a back handspring.

"What about this?" I said as I attempted a cartwheel aerial sequence.

That's how it always went. I always made new friends, even if there was initial loneliness. But how do you tell that to a young girl who is in *that moment*. A young girl who may know she will meet new friends, but just wants to fast-forward to the actual point. It's impossible to explain to the young that there are no shortcuts.

I found myself so many times in the past year wishing I could fast-forward time. Fast-forward to the place where all the boxes were emptied, and the house felt comfortable and familiar. Fast-forward to the day I wouldn't reach for the phone, wanting to call my mother, and realizing it was impossible. There were no shortcuts; one just had to cross all the roads to get to the other side.

A car honked a block away and drew me back to the present. I shook my head. "Sorry, I was a bit lost in thought. My husband's in the Navy. My father was also in the Navy, so believe it or not, I know exactly how you feel." I pointed to our porch. "Would you like to join me? What's your name?" I walked a few steps across the lawn and sat down on the steps of the porch.

"My name's Makenna," the young girl said. She carefully walked around the garden, up to the porch, and sat on the step beside me. Her hair was the color of fire and her eyes were the color of the ocean, with flecks of green.

"My name's Karen. It's nice to meet you."

Makenna smiled and looked at my garden. There wasn't much to look at, just dirt at this point.

"What are you doing?" Makenna asked.

I looked at the tree in our front yard, with its leaves overhanging, and the small space to the side, that was fully in the sun and where I hoped to make a beautiful garden full of flowers. With a few small holes and dirt everywhere, it looked quite disheveled. I tilted my head to the side to study my masterpiece. "Well, as unimpressive as it looks, I'm planting flowers." I chuckled as the words came out, because it would take a wild imagination to see my plans.

"Why?" Makenna asked. Her head tilted to the side, as she eyed the garden.

I smiled at the young girl in front of me. *There are no shortcuts.* "It goes back to when I was a little girl. Would you like me to tell you about it?"

Makenna nodded her head. "Were you my age? I'm seven." She rested her chin on her knees and looked up at me.

"Yes, I was exactly your age, and I was sad and lonely just like you."

Makenna smiled back at me. She sat up and clasped her hands together in her lap. "I want to hear the story," she said quietly.

It had been a long time since I'd told someone the story. "When I was seven we moved for the first time. I was heartbroken. I had two best friends I left behind." I looked at Makenna, sitting quietly, listening intently. "I bet you had people that you left, too."

Makenna nodded her head and moved closer to me.

"I had two best pals," she said. Her hand covered her eyes to block the sun. "I had a lot of friends in Hawaii. They all moved to Monterey when we left." She bit her lip and then squinted her eyes as if startled by the pain.

I patted her hand. "So you understand. My mom took me to the store that day and asked me to pick out flower seeds. We chose zinnias. They can withstand almost any kind of weather and they are beautiful." I picked up the envelope that the zinnia seeds came in. I held it up for her. "See, this is what the flowers will look like when they finally bloom."

"Wow," Makenna said. "They're really pretty."

I smiled at Makenna. "Yes, they are, and every time we moved, I planted zinnias with my mother. It was the one thing that became familiar and made a place home to us. And now when I move with my husband, I do the same."

Makenna looked at me, sizing me up. She opened her mouth as if to say something and then abruptly closed it. With her head down, her voice was barely audible. I leaned forward to hear her better. "Can I help you plant flowers?" she asked.

"Of course," I said. "There's a trowel hanging on the wall in there," I said as I pointed toward our garage.

For over an hour, we dug small holes in the dirt and carefully planted the seeds.

A tall woman with blond hair and a baby on her hip walked toward us. She smiled at me. "I hope Makenna wasn't any bother," she said apologetically.

I stood up and smiled at the woman. "She's no bother at all. I just moved here, and my husband is already deployed, so I enjoyed her company," I said as I gave Makenna a small pat on the back.

Her mom shifted the baby to her other hip and held out her hand. "Thank you. I'm Kelly. We'll have to have you over one night." She smiled at her daughter. "Makenna, we need to go to the store in a few minutes. Can you come home and get ready?"

"Okay, Mom." Makenna grabbed her jump rope and ran back along the sidewalk. "I made a new friend. We planted zinnias, because they can bloom anywhere."

"I see that." Kelly looked at me. "Thank you," she said.

I looked at the small girl and was filled with longing to call my own mother. I longed to tell her how much I loved her, and most of all for teaching me how to thrive like the zinnias in any kind of weather.

I looked around my neighborhood. There were people walking with their pets, and each time my eyes met someone, they smiled and waved, and it filled me with warmth.

Weeks turned into months. The house was finally settled and became a home. A place that was familiar and comfortable. I made new friends and my husband returned from his deployment. The dark funnel cloud that had accompanied the move left with the arrival of a new season.

A few months later, I saw Makenna riding her bike around the block. Two other little girls were riding behind her. Their hair blew in the wind behind them and laughter seemed to flow from them as though they didn't have a care in the world. Makenna smiled at me and waved. "I'll come visit you soon," she said.

I smiled back. "Okay, dear. I look forward to it."

She slowed her bike, and briefly stopped. Pointing at the ground she said, "Look, your flowers have bloomed."

I looked at the area she was pointing at, and there where there once had been just packed dirt, were the beautiful zinnias.

Makenna smiled at me. "Look how beautiful. They grew just like you said they would."

"Yes, Makenna, you and the flowers are thriving. We all are," I said, my voice trailing off in the wind.

SECRETS

By Jayne Ormerod

The biggest secret of my life was on the eleven o'clock news. Local investigative reporter Chuck Northwood had shown up on my front porch early this morning, tapping out an SOS on my doorbell. I'd answered the urgent summons and had been met with lights flashing and cameras rolling.

"Stella Gardner," he'd said, shoving a microphone in my face, "is it true, that you're the biological mother of Governor-Elect Richard Talbot?"

I'd slammed the door, then collapsed on the floor until Chuck and his crew gave up and left. *This can't be happening,* I thought. *Not after all these years.*

I'd hoped my lack of response had made it a non-story for ol' Chuck.

But no such luck.

Now my face, without a speck of make-up, was pixelated across my 70-inch Toshiba. *I really must get my eyes done again,* I thought.

No doubt many of my East Beach neighbors were watching it, too. How long before my doorbell rang again?

One click of the remote and Chuck faded to black.

Ding went my phone, indicating an incoming text.

Ding.

Ding.

Ding.

So many happy dings it sounded like I was in the Bellagio Casino.

Ding.

I couldn't take any more. I tossed my cell phone in the freezer and slammed the door shut.

I'd managed to keep the details of what had happened fifty-one years ago a secret. A secret I'd planned to take with me to the grave. How had Chuck Northwood, of all people, uncovered it?

June 6, 1962
East Ocean View area of Norfolk, Virginia

"Don't worry. I'll marry you."

I stared at Billy Barnes in total disbelief. "Did you just say you'd marry me?"

He nodded and then got down on one knee and pulled my hand into his. The sun was rising over the churning waters of the Chesapeake Bay. A storm was a'comin', for sure, both in the literal and figurative sense.

I heard the school bus honk its horn in the distance. That was the driver telling all the slackers to get a move on. He'd circle the bus around the small peninsula and then stop at the corner of Ocean View Avenue and 23rd Bay Street. Anyone who wasn't there could find their own way to school.

I had two minutes. I didn't want to miss it. Not today, anyway. There was something symbolic about my last school bus ride to my last day of classes at Granby High School. My life was changing in so many ways. I did not want to deal with this Billy drama this morning.

Billy cleared his throat. "Patti Jean Hollister, will you do me the honor of becoming my wife?"

"That's your solution to me being pregnant?"

He nodded again, then smiled that smile that had gotten me into my current predicament in the first place.

I yanked my hand away and fought the urge to slap his face. "Have you not been listening to me for the past two years? I have no intention of staying in this crummy, drug-infested neighborhood and raise babies while you work with your step-daddy in his painting business. I told you, Billy. I got plans. Big plans. I'm going to Hollywood and be a movie star. You heard Mr. Schnitzer tell me my interpretation of Blanche DuBois brought tears to his eyes. He said I got the 'it' factor. I'm leaving right after graduation. And ain't nobody, not Aunt Louise, not you, and especially not this baby, gonna stop me."

The school bus driver honked the horn again. I turned and trudged my way across the sand. Alone.

While my cell phone had been effectively muted, I had no such way to deal with the knocking—more like banging—on my front door. I glanced at the clock. Eleven-twenty-eight on a Friday evening. There's only one person it could be: my nosy neighbor Veronica Stanhope.

A peek through the plantation shutters confirmed it was, indeed, Veronica. She's a tall, thin woman with long blond-fading-to-gray hair that she always wore tucked into a severe bun. Despite the lateness of the evening, she was dressed in a pink sweater set and pearls, as if she were about to head off to a DAR luncheon.

She saw me and waved. As much as I wanted to, I couldn't ignore her. It just wouldn't be neighborly. So I tightened the belt on my silk robe and put on my best acting face. Let the games begin.

"Hello, Veronica," I said as I opened the door.

"Hello, Stella." Veronica pushed her way inside and walked down the hallway toward my kitchen.

I stood at the door for a moment and glanced around at the windows of all my neighbors. I noticed three instances of curtains falling shut or mini-blinds settling back into place. I guess they'd all seen the nighttime news, and probably had bets on how long it would take Veronica to come a-knockin'. Times like this I wished I lived in a remote mountain cabin and not in a community built on the concept of New Urbanism, which is all about walkable neighborhoods and adherence to strict architectural designs. Here the houses huddle close together and front porches cuddle up next to the sidewalks. That forced neighborliness, as everyone gets to know everyone else…and everyone else's business.

After closing my front door, I turned and followed

Veronica's route down the hall. My kitchen and dining room were one large space, designed in a classic "beach" feel with simple white cabinets, dark granite countertops and sea glass tchotchkes tucked in every nook and cranny. It's my favorite place to while away my retirement days.

I pulled a chair out from the long trestle table and settled in while Veronica put a kettle of water on the Viking stove to boil.

"I figure you need to talk to someone," Veronica said. "So I rushed right over, me being your best friend in the neighborhood and all..."

I guess "friendship" is in the eye of the beholder. I didn't have anyone in East Beach I considered a friend. Truth be told, there wasn't anyone in my life I considered anything more than an acquaintance. That's the price that comes with fame and fortune. And while I didn't need a friend right now, I did need someone who could help me spin the story in my favor. Yes, Veronica could prove to be very helpful. "I take it you saw the news," I said.

Veronica slipped into the seat across from me. "Is it true? Are you the biological mother of Governor-Elect Richard Talbot?"

I brushed some stray grains of salt off the table into my hand, pinched them between my thumb and forefinger and tossed them over my shoulder. *Into the face of the devil*, my Aunt Louise used to say.

Looking Veronica in the eyes, I answered her honestly. "Maybe."

June 9, 1962
East Ocean View area of Norfolk, Virginia

Aunt Louise was halfway through her second pack of cigarettes and deep into her first bottle of cheap vodka. That was a personal best for her, at least by two-thirteen on a Saturday afternoon.

"Thanks for everything," I said as I stood, suitcase in hand, by the front door of the ramshackle beach cottage I'd called home for the last twelve years of my life. After Momma and Daddy had been killed in a car accident I'd been sent here to live with Daddy's older-by-twenty-years sister. Not by choice, mind you. She was the only family member who'd take me in. She hadn't done it out of the goodness of her heart or out of a sense of family obligation. No, it had all to do with the small life insurance policy that came with me, which she blew through in three years. But by then she was legally stuck with me.

"Hey, where you goin', girl?" Aunt Louise asked in her low, gravelly voice.

"I tol' you. I'm going to Hollywood to be an actress. You'll see my name on the marquee down at The Colley Theater someday. Stella Gardner. That's gonna be my stage name." I'd spent hours practicing my autograph with a big swooping S and a lovely, grand G.

Aunt Louise's laugh sounded like a crow's cackle. "You'll be back 'fore end of summer. Ain't no way you can take care of a baby and become an actress at the same time."

"What baby?"

"Can't fool me, missy. I may be old, but I'm not blind. You got a bun in the oven."

"You're wrong, Auntie. I'm not having a baby. I'm going to Hollywood and I'm going to be a famous actress, and I'm never ever *coming back to Norfolk, Virginia. But maybe I'll send you a ticket to come see me."*

She cackled again. "Ain't no way Billy's momma's gonna let him give up that college scholarship to marry the likes of you."

"Billy's not going with me. I'm going by myself." I walked over and gave her what passed for a hug. After all, she hadn't dropped me off at St. Mary's Home for Orphans after the money ran out. It wasn't her fault she'd been born without the maternal gene.

As I stood up, I slipped a few of her sleeping pills into her bottle of vodka. I needed to buy some time to get out of town before she sent the police out after me. I was three months and two days away from being a legal adult, so technically she still had the law on her side.

The taxi was waiting for me out front. The cab driver helped me with my suitcase and I crawled in the back seat.

"To the Greyhound station, but could you circle past the Center Theater on our way, please?" Granby High School graduation would just be finishing up. It's not that I didn't want to hear the speeches encouraging us to make a mark on the world, because I'd already decided to do that. But with all that had happened in the past few days, I just couldn't work up enough enthusiasm to attend.

The driver tipped his hat to me. "Sure thing, little lady."

No tears, only sadness as we drove past the theater. My classmates and their families were all inside. Everyone but me. And Billy Barnes.

At the Greyhound station, I purchased a ticket on the first bus heading west. I could only afford to go as far as Roanoke, Virginia. Once there, I became friends with a young widow who owned The Dinner Bell Diner. She put me to work slinging hash and let me sleep in a cold, drafty room over the garage out back. She was more of a mother figure than anyone I had known in my life. She had held me when I received the news that Aunt Louise had died from a combination of sleeping pills and alcohol. And she'd helped me through my pregnancy.

Six months after I'd arrived in Roanoke, I gave birth while lying alone on a thin mattress on the floor of the garage apartment. I wrapped the baby boy in an old blanket and left him on the steps of Our Lady of Nazareth Catholic Church. I had enough money to buy a bus ticket west. This time I made it all the way to St. Louis, Missouri.

As hoped, Veronica Stanhope contacted the investigative reporter and arranged for us to meet.

Chuck Northwood now sat across from me at my large trestle table waiting for me to clarify my "Maybe" statement. The cameras were rolling, but this time I was in full make-up with styled hair and positioned so that my two Oscars and one Emmy would be in the frame. I'd been out of the spotlight for six years now, and my fans would be happy to see that Stella Gardner was aging gracefully.

Veronica flitted around in the background, making sure the gaffers and best boys sampled her home-baked chocolate-chip cookies and cream cheese-filled strawberries. I'd drawn the line at serving mimosas. This was not a party. Quite the opposite, as it was possible my world was about to spin off a cliff.

Eventually the tray of sweets made it my way, delivered by a grinning Veronica. With my stomach churning the way it was, the last thing I wanted was a goddamn cookie. But I'd cast myself in the role of a gracious Southern belle in order to get through this interview, so I took one of the thick, puffy cookies and placed it on a napkin in front of me. "Thank you kindly," I said.

After brushing a few crumbs from my fingers, I took a deep breath and turned to Chuck. "Before I answer your question, Mr. Northwood, could you do me the courtesy of telling me how you discovered my possible connection to Richard Talbot?" Oh yes, I was a very good actress indeed. My voice sounded strong and steady despite my insides jiggling like a bowl of Lila Bollinger's rainbow Jell-O salad.

"Of course." He flashed me a boyish smile and settled his forearms on my table. "It started Mother's Day last year. My gift to Mom was a Netflix subscription, and she needed help setting it up. Old dog, new tricks, and all. I cued up her selection, then stayed to watch a few minutes to make sure it was running smoothly. That movie was *Secrets*. You had me at 'Nothing makes us so lonely as our secrets.'"

Ah, yes, the opening line. I'd forgotten...

"I pulled up a recliner and stayed to watch the whole thing. You gave an amazing performance."

"Thank you." The role of Charlene Carlisle had been easy for me to play because we had so much in common, us both hiding deep, dark secrets and all.

Veronica shoved the tray of sweets under Chuck's nose. He smiled, then plucked a cream cheese-stuffed strawberry off the plate. He didn't eat it right away, but held it pinched between his thumb and forefinger as he continued speaking. "After watching *Secrets* for a second time, I became curious about your acceptance speech for your Best Actress Oscar. When I pulled the transcript, I found you thanked a woman named Gen Danvers." He popped the whole strawberry in his mouth and chewed slowly.

A cold feeling spread from my stomach up to my heart. Winning my first Oscar had been an emotional moment, and Genevieve's name had just slipped out. Of course I'd been asked by reporters and interviewers over the years, and I'd kept my story the same all along: *Gen Danvers was a woman I'd met in St. Louis who had given me the bus money to finish my journey to Los Angeles. No need to contact her, as, sadly, she'd died shortly after I'd moved west.*

"Being the investigative reporter that I am, I felt the need to track down Ms. Danvers. You had me fooled for a bit, as I thought you'd meant Jen as in Jennifer with a J, but you really meant Gen with a G for Genevieve. It took a while, but I found her, although she wasn't dead, as you'd said, nor had ever lived in St. Louis. I found her in Roanoke, Virginia, living above a diner. She's ninety-two years old now, and while she needs a walker to get around, her mind is as sharp as a tack."

Veronica plunked her treats smack dab in the middle of the table then plopped herself down right next to me. "Oh. My. God."

You'd think it was her life unraveling at the speed of light, not mine.

Chuck glanced at her and his irritation showed just a skosh before the mask of indifference slipped down over his face. He took a deep breath, then looked at me and continued his story. "Seems you left without saying a proper goodbye to Mrs. Danvers. She worried after she'd found the mattress you gave birth on, but no sign of you or the baby."

Veronica gasped. "A bay-bee. Oh. My. God."

I put my hand to my mouth, as if it alone would stop the bile churning in the back of my throat.

Chuck continued. "Not a day went by that Ms. Danvers didn't think about you, but then she sees you in a movie. *Water over the Bridge,* your first credited role. Again, a brilliant performance."

"Thank you," I whispered, no longer trusting my voice.

"Mrs. Danvers thought you had forgotten about her, until you gave that speech at the Academy Awards."

Chuck's look of censure cut me to the quick.

Guilt was a strange emotion for me and I didn't like the way I felt as it washed over me. It's true, I'd left out of Roanoke without even thanking Gen for being the mother I'd never had. No note. Not even a phone call over the years. And after all she'd done for me.

Chuck had more to say on the issue. "She told me she followed the glossy magazines, hunting for any mention of you, and more importantly any mention of your child. She was never sure if that baby had lived or died. She would like to know if he or she is all right, is all."

Gen wanted to know what happened to my baby boy. The honest-to-God truth was, I didn't know, and for fifty years hadn't cared enough to find out what had happened to the bundle I'd left on the church steps. But this afternoon I found myself caring very much, and wanting to see the boy that Billy and I had created. Was age making me nostalgic?

I rubbed my eyes and scrubbed my face, as if that would be sufficient to stop the tears that stung my eyes. Time to find out the truth. I crossed my fingers and hoped I could handle it. I leaned closer to the table and asked, "How is this all connected to Richard Talbot?"

"The Roanoke Times carried a story about a baby being left on the steps of the Catholic Church the day you left town. The baby was adopted by Marvin and Betty Talbot. I'm sure you've already figured out they named their little boy Richard."

My world spun around. My baby had a name. And a life. I took a deep breath. I'd given birth to the Governor-Elect to the state of Virginia. Another new emotion filled my heart. Momma-pride. But did I have any claim to it? No. I did not.

Chuck—and Veronica—looked at me expectantly. They wanted me to say something.

I reminded myself I was playing the role of a Southern belle, then straightened my spine and spoke in a strong clear voice. "Then you know the whole story. What more can I say?"

Despite the question having been rhetorical, Chuck had an answer. "You can tell me who the father is. Governor-Elect Talbot would like to know, and it would finish the story. I'd like to write it, if you'll let me."

It's true what they say; there are no secrets that time doesn't reveal.

The time had come for me to reveal mine. I was tired of living with it.

June 8, 1962
East Ocean View area of Norfolk, Virginia

It was long after dark before Billy walked across the dunes.

"I didn't think you were coming," I said, startling him.

He looked at me, his long bangs covering his eyes. "What are you doing here?"

"Same thing we've done every Friday night for the past three months." I smiled up at him. "You didn't think I'd miss our last time out before graduation, did you?"

"I don't get you, Patti Jean. You laugh off my proposal of marriage, yet here you are."

"Here" was on the dunes of the Chesapeake Bay, hunkered down by an old, wooden rowboat. During one of our moonlit walks on the beach we'd stumbled upon it. We'd watched it for a few weeks, and when nobody seemed to claim it, we took it out for a spin on the bay. It had become our Friday Night Date, weather permitting, of course. Billy would row us out and we'd float and talk and do other stuff and then return it to its spot on the dunes. Nobody had ever seemed to care. We'd even christened our little boat Bay Dreams, because we dreamed of our future while out on the bay.

"I'm real sorry about Wednesday morning," I said as I moved closer and slipped my arms around his waist. "I wasn't ready for you to be sweet about it. I don't want this baby to ruin both of our lives."

"It won't ruin anything," Billy said. "Just change things a little." His arms snaked around me.

"More like a lot!"

"I'm serious, Patti Jean. I want to marry you. I really do. I'd much rather be with you than go off to William and Mary. I won't fit in there. We both know that."

Billy was smart. Real smart. He'd picked up a full scholarship to one of the oldest and best schools in Virginia. His momma and step-daddy were so proud. They'd kill him if he gave up the chance for a successful future to marry me.

And he would, too. Give up everything for me and the baby. Way I saw it, there was only one way for me to make sure that didn't happen.

Billy bent his head and kissed me. "It'll be okay, Pattie Jean. I promise."

"If you say so," I said. "Come on, let's get this boat out. We can talk while we're floating." Floating on the bay while the moon shimmered off the water was one of my favorite things to do. "And I brought something to drink. Your favorite." Vodka, stolen from Aunt Louise's stash, and orange juice, lifted from the corner market.

We dragged the boat to the shore, and I climbed in, dragging my bag of stuff with me. I reached my hand in as one last check to make sure I had everything I needed: vodka, orange juice, glasses, and rope.

I mixed up a strong drink and passed it to Billy. He drained the glass and tossed it back to me. Then he started rowing. Soon we were far off shore so that we felt like the only two people on earth. Billy downed his drinks as fast as I passed them to him. He kept rowing, but his movements were becoming slow and muddled. Good. That was the most important part of my plan.

We talked, Billy and me, about everything from math class to our options for the future. All the time I kept pouring more drinks for us. Only mine were pure orange juice while Billy's were mostly vodka.

The moon rose over the water and Billy stretched out on the seat. Didn't take long until he was good and passed out.

I grabbed the rope and tied up Billy's hands and feet. At the end I tied the small boat's anchor, which was heavier than I'd thought. Perfect. With great effort, I rolled him out of the boat and watched him sink beneath the surface of the Chesapeake Bay.

It took me almost an hour to row my way back to shore. I left the boat in the water and gave it a good push toward the east where it would be carried out to the Atlantic and disappear forever. Then I walked the two blocks home and snuck back through my bedroom window. I needn't have bothered being so furtive because when I peeked out to the den I saw Aunt Louise still snoozing on the sofa.

The boat floated to shore the next day, but Billy's body was never found.

I gazed at my grown son through the plexi-glass that separated us at the Norfolk Jail. He had his father's strong build and charismatic smile. But he had my expressive green eyes. I felt a sense of pride that warmed my heart more than all of my theatrical awards combined. My son, my baby boy, was the Governor-Elect of Virginia. There was even a little Presidential buzz. I could be the mother of a U. S. President.

No, wait. That was Betty Talbot's title. She'd raised him to be this fine, principled man.

I'd only given birth to him. Had I tried to raise him myself, he'd have been the son of a house painter, whose mother had learned everything she'd known about mothering from her alcoholic aunt. We'd have lived in a tiny run-down beach cottage by the Chesapeake Bay, and he could have easily been sucked into the underground world of drugs and crime. Instead, he'd been raised privileged, with the best education money could buy. And he'd been loved. After sixty-eight years on earth, that's the one thing I'd never learned to do. I'd never learned to love.

I saw his mouth moving but didn't catch what he said. "What?" I asked, leaning closer to the plastic that separated us.

"I asked, was it worth it?"

I had a brief flash of memory of my time in Hollywood as an A-list celebrity for almost thirty years. The glitz, the glamour, the parties, the world-travel, and the adoring fans. But the best part was the money. More money than I could spend in one lifetime. Little Pattie Jean Hollister from East Ocean View had found fame and fortune as Stella Gardner, just as I'd told Aunt Louise I would.

I repeated Richard's question in my mind. *Had it been worth it?*

I looked at my son through the glass. Governor-Elect Richard Talbot.

Had it been worth it?

If I were to be honest, yes.

THE SNIPER SISTERS

By Jayne Ormerod

"It's my turn to pull the trigger." Evie slipped the gearshift of her navy blue Club Car into reverse and stomped down on the accelerator. The upscale golf cart shot out of the garage and into the alley.

Her older-by-three-minutes sister Dot grabbed onto the support bar and managed, barely, to remain in her seat. "No, you knocked off Marty Knudsen last week, remember?"

"Of course I remember," Evie snarled as she switched into forward gear. Again she slammed the accelerator while quickly tugging the steering wheel to the left. "Direct hit to his heart. But you got the three before that."

"Only because your shot at Alma Schaeffer went wide and took out Cuddles McGee instead."

"It didn't go wide. I meant to shoot that damn cat. It'd left two more goldfinches on my doorstep that morning."

Dot struggled to stay in her seat and hold onto her

gun as Evie took the turn onto 28th Bay Street on two wheels. "If I hadn't acted quickly to take Alma out, she would have gotten us first. You were taking too long to reload. Not my fault you screwed up your opportunity."

"Not gonna argue with you, sis. I'm making this hit today because I'm a better shot than you."

"No, not better. Just luckier."

"Luckier, my Aunt Gertrude!" The cart roared onto the green at the north end of 28th Bay Street and Evie slammed on the brakes. The Club Car shuddered to a stop. "That was pure huntress skill that took down Bertie Haversham," she said.

Dot dismissed Evie's success as if swatting at a pesky gnat. "Heck, even blindfolded you'd have hit Bertie's broad behind."

"Are you the pot or the kettle here?" Evie crossed her arms and stared pointedly at Dot's desert cammies, stretched to within a stitch of their lives.

"At least I have the good sense not to bend over to pull weeds from my garden. Talk about an irresistible target—"

"What about Hank, then?" Evie struggled to get out from behind the wheel. "One bullet and he was a goner."

"He was snoring in his hammock. There's no skill involved in hitting a stationary target." Dot used her shirt sleeve to mop her brow. "Let's get moving." She pushed her pith helmet lower on her gray curls, then turned and climbed out of the cart. She set off north along the overgrown path that led to the shore of the Chesapeake Bay, using the butt of her gun as a machete to swat away leggy sea oats.

Evie marched along in her sister's wake. "Charlie knows we're after him, and he'll be on heightened alert. We won't get a second shot at him, either. I still think I should do the hit."

"You know it's personal for me. Charlie cheated me out of a dollar seventy-five last week at the Canasta tournament. Nobody cheats Dot Westmoreland and gets away with it."

"Your husband cheated—"

Dot waved her gun over her head. "Possession is nine-tenths, sister dear. I'm shooting today. And any more yapping and we'll miss our chance at Charlie. Now hush or he'll hear us coming."

Dusk was descending and the beach was deserted. The only sound was that of the waves lapping gently on the shore. Keeping as low as their 70-year-old knees would allow, they snuck along the sand dunes that separated the bay from the East Beach neighborhood. Three blocks later, they stopped and dropped onto the sand.

A seagull found a discarded sandwich and sent out a notice to all other birds in the area.

"Hell's bells. Might as well send up flares," Dot said.

Evie ignored her sister's grumbles. She always got testy before a kill.

They lowered themselves onto to their bellies and crawled like G. I. Janes to the top of the dune. Rosemary Weatherly's cedar-shingled cottage sat on the other side of a white picket fence, less than fifty yards away.

Evie tapped the face of her watch with her gnarled finger. "In exactly three minutes, Charlie should be coming out from that door. He'll walk along the porch, then down the green to the beach access path and stop there," she said while pointing to a spot five feet from where they hid. "He'll dispose of the evidence in the trashcan. You'll have to catch him before he turns away and heads back to the houses. He's got a grudge match set with Old Man Gunderson in an eight-ball tournament and he'll be in a hurry to get there."

"Good reconnaissance, Evie."

"Thanks, Dot, but next time you can help Rosemary make two-hundred and seventy-nine fruitcakes. Do you know how much candied fruit has to be chopped in order to make two-hundred and seventy-nine fruitcakes? All just to find out about her and Charlie's secret rendezvous." Evie flexed her gnarled fingers. The pain still lingered five days later.

"I can't believe Charlie would go to so much trouble just to sneak a Big Mac and a chocolate shake every week. If the good Lord sees fit to keep me on this earth until I'm eighty-seven years old, well, I'm gonna eat whatever I want whenever I want and I don't care who sees me."

"Amen to that, sister." Evie removed the lens cap from her bird-watching glasses. Periscoping her head above the dune, she focused in on Rosemary Weatherly's wide southern porch. "You know something, Dot? I haven't felt this alive in fifty-odd years. Kind of makes me regret a lifetime of organizing bake sales and attending civic league meetings when I could have been a CIA agent or something."

"He's coming. Get down," Dot said as she swung her legs around until she lay flat on her stomach. She poked the barrel of her gun through the sea oats. With one eye closed, she stared through the viewfinder. Slowly and deliberately, she fit her finger into the gun's trigger mechanism.

Evie wiped the sweat beading on her brow. She was certain the thundering of her heart would give away their position.

"I've got him in my sights," Dot whispered as her finger twitched on the trigger. "Come on, Charlie. Come to Mama."

The two women watched Charlie shuffle down the brick path. He took one final slurp of his milkshake before tossing the cup in the trash can. A satisfied smile spread across his face.

"Now!" Evie hissed.

Dot applied firm and steady pressure to the trigger. With a loud crack, the gun fired.

The two women waited just long enough to see a crimson stain spread down Charlie's white golf shirt before they turned and scampered back along the beach. It wasn't until their electric cart was skittering down the alley behind their house that Evie dared to speak. "Nice shot, Dot."

"Thank you, Evie."

That evening, conversation at the First Friday potluck at the Bay Front Club focused on the assassination of one of their neighbors.

"Poor Charlie never knew what hit him."

"I heard tell that Rosemary set him up."

"'Bout time somebody took that Canasta-cheatin' son of a biscuit-maker out."

As diners scooped up the last morsels of their Key lime pie, Georgia Davidson, the social director, made her way to the front of the room. The microphone let out a terrible squeak as she started to speak. "Ladies and Gentlemen. I'm sure you've all heard of Charlie Cavanaugh's assassination this afternoon." An excited murmur rippled across the crowd. "A fitting ending for a courageous player. He was the last living member of the infamous Go Ahead, Make My Day team, shot at five forty-three this afternoon. Let's have a hand for Charlie." Her arm swept toward the back of the room where Charlie slumped in a metal chair.

The crowd rose and gave him a standing ovation. Charlie acknowledged their acclamation with a wave of his hand.

Georgia waited until the audience settled back down before continuing. "It's with great pleasure that I award this year's Paintball Assassination Game championship trophy to The Sniper Sisters, Dorothy Westmoreland and Evelyn Binghamton. Congratulations, ladies, for a game well played."

HERBIE MEETS HIS MATCH

BY MIKE OWENS

It could have worked out if she'd been more specific, hadn't waffled about when he pressed for a commitment. Herbie needed commitment. He needed boundaries, time lines. He couldn't work with "We'll see," or, worse yet, "Maybe." What the hell did that mean, anyway? What if an umpire said, "Maybe that was strike three," or "Maybe you're out"? Maybe was the worst word in the language. Maybe was chaos. Maybe was verbal anarchy. Every time she said the word, he ground a little more enamel off his molars. A romance was either on or off, just like an appliance. There was no maybe about it. So he had to cut her loose. He sent her an e-mail.

And it wasn't just her. The whole country was in on it. Maybe, maybe, maybe. Maybe your flight would arrive on time. Maybe you'd get that delivery today, maybe tomorrow, maybe never. Standards, that's what the world needed, standards and consequences. But enough of that. Now he needed a replacement woman.

The new girl, Anna from accounting, the one he'd

met at the quarterly staff meeting last week, would she work out better? At least he'd never heard an accountant say maybe. She seemed organized. That was good. There was the issue of her last name—Italian, too many Ns and Os, and they seemed to be arranged oddly as if someone put letters in a box, shook it and whatever came out was her last name. No last name should ever have more than five letters.

She was, as they say, built. That was good, too. He was quite fond of large bosoms, not too large, mind you, just large enough. Her eyebrows were a bit too bushy for his taste, sort of like a lawn that needed edging, but her bosom cancelled that out.

She'd made a move on him right off. She dropped by his office to ask about a payroll issue and ended up asking him over for dinner. That was good. No wasted motion, none of that random activity people called courtship. And she looked him straight in the eye. That was good. In his "pass-fail" system, she rated a solid pass.

Dinner at her place that evening. With Herbie's system, getting ready for a first date would be no more complicated than getting ready for work. He shaved, then showered, never the other way around. He draped the towel over the rod, careful that the dangling ends matched up so they would dry evenly.

Choosing something to wear took no time at all. Organization was the key, and he had his closet sectioned off so that slacks hung separately from dress shirts, dress shirts separate from casuals. Jeans were folded and stacked on the shelf alongside—but not touching— sweaters, cottons and wools in separate stacks, of course.

He kept his jackets in another closet, arranged in descending order with newest/most expensive on the far left, ending with his oldest, slightly threadbare coats on the far right. For a first date he always chose something from the middle.

What would she be serving for dinner? Pasta most likely. Not his favorite. He didn't mind the taste, he just preferred his food items separate. He hated it when the mashed potatoes slopped over into the green beans, or worse still, when there was some kind of gravy that got into everything. And pasta, forget about it.

That sort of thing didn't happen in his kitchen. He had a supply of cafeteria-style plates, the ones with the compartments set off by ridges. Everything stayed just where it was supposed to be.

"I live in East Beach," she'd said. "A new condo, right on Pretty Lake Avenue." She had drawn him a map.

Herbie had watched her walk away, purposeful, just the right amount of motion. Yes. He'd made a mental note to put a check mark on his list beside WALK. Then he'd written the date and time on the map, made a copy, and filed away the original in the cabinet beside his desk.

The drive from his apartment to East Beach took about twenty minutes. He allowed thirty, which gave him time to look around. Where she lived would count a lot toward her success—or failure—as his replacement woman.

Herbie was impressed. Now this, he thought as he drove down a tree-lined lane, was how a community should be. The homes were all similar, yet each was unique in its own way. There was none of the cookie-cutter look that he found so distasteful in most new communities. Small, neatly trimmed lawns, no wasted space. Herbie hated wasted space.

As he drove along, several people strolling waved to him. Herbie didn't wave back. He didn't know these people. He rolled up his car windows and checked to see that his doors were all locked. Perhaps these wavers were just being friendly, but you never could be too careful.

His tour came to an end when he realized it was almost seven, and he was lost. Only the most desperate circumstances could have forced him to do what he did next; he stopped a passing jogger and asked for directions.

"Pretty Lake? Sure. Turn here, then go down this street about four blocks or so. You'll turn right onto Pretty Lake Avenue. Can't miss it." Then the jogger waved and trotted off.

Herbie quickly rolled his window back up and drove away. He parked across the street from Anna's condo. Very nice, he thought. Entirely suitable. One more point for Anna.

Inside, a uniformed security guard put down his newspaper and smiled up at Herbie. "Nice evening, isn't it?" he asked.

But Herbie wasn't one for idle banter. "Anna Bonnifaccio, unit two-oh-three," he said.

"Okay, if you'll just sign in here. Elevator is on your right."

She met him at the door wearing an apron that looked like she'd worn it in a paint ball attack. When he didn't move, she took his arm and pulled him inside.

"What's wrong?" she asked.

"Your apron. Were you injured?"

"Oh, you are too funny." She kissed him on the cheek. "I'm a bit of a slob when I cook. You should see my stove, or, maybe you shouldn't. Come on in. I have to run back to the kitchen."

Herbie checked out her living room. Not good. The furniture arrangement was completely out of balance, too many big pieces on one side. The room looked lopsided. Probably it was too early to make suggestions about changing it; he'd discuss it with her later. He took a pillow off the sofa, fluffed it and coughed when the cloud of dust flew in his face.

"Are you okay in there?"

"Yeah. Just a little cough, nothing serious."

She emerged from the kitchen carrying two glasses of red wine. "Have a seat," she said.

Herbie moved to the other end of the sofa, away from the dusty pillow.

"Oh, no, not there. You'll crush Biscuit."

Herbie bolted up from his half-crouch. "Biscuit? Why is there bread on your sofa?" This couldn't be good.

"Biscuit isn't a real biscuit. She's my kitten." She handed Herbie his wine and directed him to an armchair. "You really are too funny. I love a man with a sense of humor."

She'd taken off the spattered apron revealing a clingy blue dress that shimmered as she moved. That was good. It cancelled out the unbalanced room, almost.

"You look great." Herbie sipped his wine.

"Thanks."

"Where were you before, before accounting, I mean?"

"I was with another company."

Herbie waited but she said no more about it.

"I guess you've worked at Peabody's for a long time," she said.

"Eleven years."

"Wow. I've never worked anywhere that long."

"Why not?" He didn't mean to be so blunt, but there it was. He couldn't very well take it back now.

"I like new things, new experiences."

New things? New meant change. That was not good. It wasn't good because change meant risk, and there was nothing to be gained from taking risk. Why on earth would anybody want to take risks?

A little bell sounded in the kitchen. Anna jumped up. She waggled her finger at him. "Come with me. Dinner is ready."

"What are we having?"

"You'll see."

"Could I wash up first?"

"Right through there. Don't be long."

Ah ha, the bathroom. He learned a lot from bathrooms. He turned on the water, then made a quick inspection. First, the tub. No ring. That was good. Toilet? Clean. Very good. Final test, the medicine cabinet. Ugh. A disaster. Old pill bottles, a half-empty toothpaste tube missing its cap, old makeup stuff. She must have crammed everything in there before he came. This was not good.

So far, the evening was going less well than he'd

hoped: one positive—the clingy blue dress—and three negatives, four if he counted the medicine cabinet.

"I was beginning to think I'd have to come and get you." She took his arm and pulled him toward the table.

"Sorry," Herbie said.

"Have a seat. I hope you brought along a good appetite."

It was hopeless. He could see that before he even sat down. The veal parmigiana covered more than half his plate, overlapped with a big dollop of pasta, both of them submerged beneath a sea of lumpy red sauce. A lonely nest of zucchini huddled in the corner trying to escape the creeping sauce.

Anna stood behind him and tied a red bib around his neck. "Don't want you to mess up that pretty shirt."

He tried in vain to separate his dinner components, but as soon as he pushed apart the veal and the pasta they slid back together again. The sauce was the major culprit. If he could just scoop it all up on top of the veal...but that didn't work either. The sauce had a mind of its own, a mandate to cover everything on his plate.

"What on earth are you doing?" Anna asked.

"I'm just...ouch." Something was climbing up his leg, something with very sharp claws.

"What's wrong? You're really acting weird."

"Your cat's in my lap."

"Oh, for heaven's sake. Biscuit come here." She walked to Herbie's side and retrieved the cat. "Biscuit loves my pasta sauce, don't you, Baby?" She held the cat close and nuzzled it. Biscuit began licking Anna's lips. She sneezed, and Biscuit twisted out of her grasp. The cat landed squarely in the middle of Herbie's plate, slipped in the sauce, rolled over, then leapt onto Herbie's shoulder.

This was not good. Herbie tried to remove the sopping Biscuit, but the cat dug her claws deeply into his jacket. "Help me," he said.

But Anna, now doubled over with laughter, was no help at all.

"Not funny," Herbie said. "This is not funny."

Anna lost her balance, and fell backwards onto the floor, still laughing.

Herbie moved away from the table and bent over, his head close to the floor. Surely the cat would get the message and jump off his shoulder. Instead, Biscuit ascended to Herbie's now highest point, his butt.

"Oh, Herbie. You've got a cat stuck to your ass." Anna lay flat on the floor, red faced and wheezing. "I'm sorry," she said. "You are the funniest man I've ever met."

Funny? This woman probably found train wrecks hilarious. Meanwhile Biscuit had dug his claws deeply into Herbie's left butt cheek.

When Anna finally struggled to her feet, she gathered up the cat, allowing Herbie to stand upright. She didn't seem to mind that the sauce-coated cat smeared red goo all over her dress. Now the appearance of her apron was starting to make sense. This woman was clearly dangerous.

"Come into the bathroom, and I'll clean you up," she said.

Bathroom? No way. He'd barely survived her kitchen. She might be lethal in the bathroom. "I'd better go."

"No, please, I'm really sorry." She took his arm. "Besides, you can't go out like that. You look like a big, squashed tomato." More laughter. She held onto a chair for support.

Biscuit looked like she might make a leap for his shoulder. Herbie bolted for the door. He almost ran over the white-haired lady passing in the hallway.

"Ohmigod, you poor man. I'll call nine-one-one." The lady in the hall flattened herself against the wall, far away from Herbie and the red tide that covered him.

"No, it's okay. It's just catsup," he said. "A practical joke."

He took the stairs and headed for the front door.

"Hold on there." The security guard now blocked the front entrance, his left hand held up in a stop-traffic position.

Herbie stopped short. He probably looked like a novice axe murderer fleeing the crime scene. "It's just spaghetti sauce." He ran his finger through the slippery substance that coated his neck and part of his head, then popped it into his mouth. "See? You wanna taste it?"

"Sauce?" The guard lowered his left hand but kept his right firmly on his firearm.

"A little disagreement," Herbie said. He couldn't go into the whole story—the cat, Anna rolling on the floor. He didn't even want to think about it.

"I still have to sign you out." The guard moved back to his desk and flipped the log book around. "Your name?"

"Herb Claussen. I was visiting two-oh-three."

"Two-oh-three? Oh, yeah, you were visiting Anna?"

Herbie nodded, and the sauce oozed down inside his collar.

"Anna did this?"

"It was an accident," Herbie said.

The guard pounded his desk. His laughter reverberated through the vestibule. "Anna. I'll have to watch out for that lady." He took off his glasses and rubbed his eyes. "Oh, boy, she sure made a mess out of you."

"Yeah, thanks."

Herbie sauntered to his car, hands in his pockets, whistling, not a care in the world. Why, he poured spaghetti sauce on his head several times a week, nothing unusual, nothing at all.

Some snickered, some recoiled as if in horror. But no one in the parking lot approached him, except for the little girl who pulled away from her mom and ran up to him. She eyed him, her head cocked to one side. "What happened to you?"

Herbie stood straight, squared his shoulders, and put on his best stern face. "This, little girl, is what can occur when you don't keep your food groups separate. Remember that."

By the time he got home, the pasta sauce had undergone several changes in consistency from viscous liquid to a thick paste to the final horror he now faced, a plaque-like semi-solid caked to his head and neck. He tossed his shirt and jacket into the trash. Both were beyond salvation. He stood under the shower with rivulets of red running down his torso. Would he be normal after all the sauce was gone? Would there be any permanent damage? This was a trial the likes of which he hadn't faced before. He couldn't very well go through life with a red head and neck, like a wingless woodpecker.

Damn that woman and her sauce and her bushy eyebrows. She was a menace, a public health hazard. But better he found out about her sooner rather than later, before he'd made any kind of emotional investment in a relationship. So far, it had cost him a shirt and a jacket, not to mention the humiliation, but it could have been worse, much worse.

After a long soak and much soaping, he dried himself off and checked himself in the mirror in his bedroom. As far as he could tell, he remained unscarred, only the internal wounds to deal with.

Herbie fixed himself a light dinner of two boiled eggs. Boiling them allowed easy separation of the whites from the yellow centers. He rewarded himself with a beer; he'd come through a significant trial and lived to tell the tale, not that he ever would.

He dropped his fork…she wouldn't tell, would she? Would he be facing smirks and behind-his-back laughter at work the next day? Damn. He'd have to be much more careful about his social contacts.

Even with the clear and present danger Anna posed, she kept popping into his mind—that clingy blue dress, the way her eyes danced when she laughed. With the right coaching might she be transformed into someone more acceptable, someone who appreciated the value of "A place for everything and everything in its place?" Was he the man for the job?

He strode into the office the next morning, the picture of command and confidence, a confidence he really didn't feel. The first giggle would probably fracture his façade, but none came. Just the usual chorus of "Good morning, Mr. Claussen."

The gift-wrapped box on his desk was tucked off to one side, not easily visible, so probably few had seen it. There was a card held in place by the white ribbon.

"Dear Herbie, please forgive. If you're not too angry, I'd love to try again. Anna."

Why, such presumption. Who did she think he was? After she'd laughed at his agony. Funny. She thought he was funny. He'd had been called lots of things in his life, but funny was not on the list. She wanted another chance? By God, he'd give her a chance. He'd give her a lot more than a chance. By the time he was through with her she'd shine like a polished gem.

"So, I'll pick you up at seven?" he asked.

"Oh, yes. I'm just so happy you're not still angry with me."

Anna extended her hand and somehow, without thinking, he took it. Warmth traveled from his fingertips through his arm and into his chest. Whoa. This wouldn't do, not at all, holding hands in the office. What kind of an example was he setting? This was not good. He stepped back. "Seven, then," he said, but it came out weak, with none of the authority he tried to project when he made appointments.

He went back to his office and closed the door, just as the warmth spread up into his face. A few deep breaths, nothing he couldn't handle. Everything was under control.

He planned carefully. Pick her up at seven, dinner at seven-thirty. The restaurant he chose was French; portions would be small, no problem with things getting all mixed together, and if she spilled anything, the mess would be modest. Anna didn't know it yet, but her education was about to begin.

Splendid, just splendid. She was such a good student, but then, he was an excellent teacher. The dinner exceeded his expectations, so much progress so soon. Had he missed something? He found so little to correct. Why, his influence must be much greater than he had imagined. Already she was following his example.

There was some problem with concentration, the way her eyes caught the glow of the candlelight and the soft melody of her laughter, not the raucous bark he'd had to endure on their first date. Yes indeed, she showed promise. His task was keeping his goal in sight, creation of an orderly, precise, specific Anna, an Anna who, in many ways, resembled himself. Was that too much to hope for?

When she went to the powder room, he pulled the list from his pocket. Out of ten items he'd targeted for correction, he put check marks beside eight. Eight in only one hour. The last two he'd have to assess later. He was doing so well. Perhaps he'd missed his calling. Should he consider a career as some kind of motivational coach?

He watched her walk back to the table, and he caught the sidelong glances of men at other tables. Let them look. She was coming back to his table, to sit with him. His chest swelled a bit. No, no, no. He had a job to do. He had no time for such feelings. Still, when he stood to hold her chair, she smiled, and his knees got all spindly.

"This is such a lovely place, Herbie. Thanks so much for bringing me here."

She placed her hand over his, and the now-familiar warmth coursed through his body. What on earth was going on?

"My pleasure," he said. He grabbed for his water glass and knocked it over. Ohmigod. He hadn't spilled a water glass since he was a child. What would she think? What kind of example was he setting?

"Oops," she said. Her soft laughter flowed across the table. "No problem."

And she was right. Their waiter materialized, as French waiters do, and placed a couple of extra napkins on the spill. It was nothing, after all.

"Would monsieur like another bottle of wine?" the waiter asked as he refilled their glasses.

Another bottle? Meaning they'd finished a bottle

already? How could that be? He'd monitored Anna's intake glass by glass. It was all on his checklist. But he hadn't counted his own. He glanced at Anna. She shook her head, the picture of decorum. "No, thanks," he said.

He raised his glass and touched hers. "To a lovely evening," he said.

She nodded.

She closed her eyes as she sipped her wine and, while she did, he spilled half his glass on his shirt. Ohmigod. He'd done it again. What was happening to him? Herbie the slob. This was wrong, all wrong. And there it was again, her soft laughter.

"Herbie, whatever am I going to do with you?" she asked.

The waiter, as if he were anticipating something of the sort, arrived with a bottle of soda water. He poured some onto a napkin and handed it to Herbie.

"Here, I'll do that." Anna moved her chair around next to him and blotted the wine on his shirt. "I'm not sure this will work completely," she said. "I'm making a terrible mess of your wardrobe."

What did it matter? She was close beside him, touching him. He had other shirts.

MILLIE'S MISSING KEY

By Jenny F. Sparks

"Use your noodle, Doodle!" That is my person, Jenny. She likes to rhyme all the time. Oh good grief! Seems I do, too. I am Millie, the golden doodle. We just finished our daily walk here in beautiful East Beach. A warm breeze is blowing off the Chesapeake Bay. I like these days because we walk longer. When we got back home this morning, Jenny reached in her pocket to pull out our house key. She made a face. No key! We sit on the stoop of our town home together. I put my chin on her lap and she scratches the buff colored curls on my head. I don't mind.

"Do you think I forgot them? Oh, that doesn't make sense. We are locked out, which means the key is out, too." She talks to me a lot. I wish I could tell her I understand her when she talks to me. But, I have to settle for barks and tail wags. "Shoot! I wish Mike would let me keep a key in the planter. I used to do that all of the time when he was deployed, and we lived in Florence." She lets out a long sigh.

I look up and see my friend, Max, the Jack Russell terrier, walking down the street. His tiny person is named Sarah. He doesn't like her very much yet. She cries a lot. I told him she is just new and doesn't know how to be in the world yet. Eliza is his grown up person. She tries to give him attention, but the baby takes a lot of her time these days. Max gets mad and growls and acts ugly.

"I don't suppose you came across a key on your walk?" Jenny asks Eliza.

"No key so far. But I'll keep my eyes out for it."

"How is Sarah today?" Jenny asks as she leans over the side of the carriage. Jenny makes goofy faces at Sarah while she and Eliza catch up. Getting a grandbaby is top on Jenny's wish list. I wonder if I will feel like Max does if we do get a grandbaby.

"Are you headed toward the park? We'll walk along with you, if you don't mind."

"Sure, come on," replies Eliza.

When we get to the park, other families are there, too. Mommies push toddlers on swings or sit on the bench with the little babies. There are some other dogs there, too. A big black poodle named Pierre bounds up and almost knocks Sarah out of her carriage. Max starts barking and snapping at Pierre to get him to go away. I look at Max and say, "See, I knew you loved her."

We visit for a while, then Jenny looks at me and says, "All right, Girly-que, let's keep looking." We continue on our do-over walk. I'm game. I like to walk because I get to see my friends. And we live near the beach so I get to smell all kinds of good smells. I found a crab once when we were on the beach. It didn't end so well for me. Jenny had to pull it off my nose. I guess some things don't need to be sniffed.

We turn the corner at the pretty house with a white picket fence. There is my friend, Zuzu, the yellow Lab. I like to see her. Sometimes she will play with me. Mostly, she sits on her porch and lets me hang out in her yard while Jenny and her person talk or work on their crafts. I like the sound of Zuzu's person's voice. She sounds like the people where my Grammie lives in South Carolina. I think she's from there, too.

"Hey, there, Zuzu! We're back. Have you seen a key on a blue keychain?" Jenny talks to all dogs the way she talks to me. Zuzu cocks her head and looks at Jenny like she is a goon. Maybe I'm the only dog who understands what she is saying.

Slam! The screen door swings shut as Willa walks out onto the porch. "Didn't we just see you two?"

"My house key is MIA. Have you seen it? It's on the key chain with blue beads and palmetto trees on it."

"Is that the one I gave you? No, I haven't seen it."

"It is. It's my favorite. Reminds me of home and the fun I had in DC at the Family Line office." Jenny and Willa met in DC when they both volunteered with other navy spouses.

"Zuzie is too old to walk anymore. But, I'll keep an eye out for it. Do you need a bottle of water while you look?" Southern hospitality—you can take the girl out of the south but not the south out of the girl.

"That would be great. Thanks." Willa dashes inside

to fetch the bottle of water while Jenny rubs Zuzu's back.

Water in hand, we set off again. We trace our footsteps past the pastel houses on 24th Bay. The one next to Zuzu has a big lady fish in the front yard. I think they call it a mermaid. It feels like she stares at me when we walk past, so I go faster. There is a little yippy dog barking from behind one of gates. As we get closer to the beach, a black and brown dog comes into view. She sees us, too, points her nose to the sky and tries to bark. That's Jamaica. She is old, too, and can't always bark. She goes through the motions, but no sound comes out. It's kinda funny.

Jenny waves at the lady with Jamaica. "Hi, Jayne! How's it going?"

"I'm great." Jayne reaches down to scratch my chin. "Hello Miss Millie. How is the world's cutest puppy?" I like Jayne.

"I don't suppose you have come across a keychain with a single key on it?" Jenny is busy trying to pet Jamaica. But Jamaica is still trying to warn the world that we are coming. Eventually, she gets tired and sinks down on the sidewalk. Jenny plops down beside her and finally gets a scratch in.

"Nope, no key. But, I will look for it. Are you coming to play this afternoon?"

"I will if I find my key and get a shower." Jenny smiles at Jayne. "And I'm bringing my new Mah Jongg set. I can't wait to use it. It's neat knowing Toni learned to play on it." Toni is their friend who just retired to North Carolina.

As the ladies talk, I lie down near Jamaica. A low

growl emits from her snout but she doesn't move. I slide one paw forward and whimper my best puppy whine. Jamaica raises an eyebrow but doesn't move. I slide a little closer to her. More growling but she holds her ground. Finally I get close enough to give her a big Millie kiss. Mission accomplished. I lie down to keep her company.

"OK, Sweetie. Let's keep going."

We cross the dunes by the Bay Front Club onto the beach of the Chesapeake Bay. I like the beach. I pull at my leash, and Jenny lets me off of it. I gallop as fast as I can toward the water to chase the waves, and stop short. Several seagulls screech and take off in my direction. I turn and hightail it back to Jenny.

"Scaredy-cat. Errr. Scaredy-dog."

Off we trot down the beach, keeping a watchful eye for crabs and seagulls. Who knew the beach could be so full of challenges? We continue our search and listen as the waves lap on the shore. Jenny keeps looking out at the water, watching for navy ships. My man person is on one of them somewhere far away. When we are on the beach, Jenny feels close to him. We cut back through the dunes and into the neighborhood.

"Hello, friend." A familiar voice calls out. It's our friend, Clark, and his dog, Comet, the Irish setter. Comet prances toward us. He is always full of energy. We give each other the obligatory sniff and then start playing chase.

"How's it going, Clark?"

"Doing good. How about you?"

"We're on our second walk of the day, searching for my lost house key. Aren't you getting ready to take a trip?"

"That's right. We are headed to Ireland this time. I will think of you when we are in the pubs."

"Have one for me."

"Of course. Good luck with the key."

"Thanks."

We finish our walk for the second time and plop down on the porch again. I put my head on my paws to rest when something shiny catches my eye. I scooch over a bit and tug on Jenny's shoe. Jenny stares down at her feet and sighs. "Oh, good grief! I forgot I did that! Good eye, Millie!" There is the key tied to Jenny's sneaker. She had gotten tired of juggling the key chain, leash, and the clean-up-after-your-pet bag. So she resorted to her old college habit.

"Well, Miss Millie, I guess we got our ten thousand steps in today."

ABOUT THE AUTHORS

GINA WARREN BUZBY is originally from Columbia, SC. She has a B.A. in Art from Columbia College and a Masters from Clemson University. Currently, Gina serves on these boards: Columbia College, Armed Services YMCA/Hampton Roads, East Beach Writers Guild and The Tidewater Collection at Norfolk Naval Base. Gina is also a member of P.E.O. - Philanthropic Educational Organization, Chapter AK. Gina works as a Fine Artist from her home studio in East Beach. She enjoys teaching the "Van Gogh and Vino" classes at the East Beach Sandwich Company and through private bookings. View her paintings via her website www.GinaWarrenBuzby.com.

PATRICK CLARK was born in Milwaukee, Wisconsin. He is a graduate of the School of Journalism at the University of Wisconsin – Milwaukee and holds a Master of Arts degree in National Security and Strategic Studies from the U.S. Naval War College. Patrick earned a commission in the United States Navy where he served as a Surface Warfare Officer. He retired after twenty years of service, went into industry as a Vice President of Operations, and retired after thirteen years. His writing themes leverage his knowledge of the military and government to develop stories with suspense and intrigue. He currently lives in Norfolk, Virginia. Website: www.patrick-clark.com.

MICHELLE DAVENPORT is a stay-at-home navy wife currently living in Norfolk, VA. A transplant from southern Illinois, Michelle spends her days taking care of her two cats, dog, and bird as well as her loving husband. When not caring for her little family, she enjoys volunteering, reading, and catching up with friends. Blog: www.michelleddavenport.blogspot.com.

KAREN HARRIS is a writer and editor from San Francisco, California. As the wife of a naval officer, she has lived in Japan and all over the eastern half of the United States. She and her husband have two children and call Virginia Beach, Virginia home

WILL HOPKINS lives in East Beach. He is the author of three police mysteries set in mid-century Norfolk: *Willowood, Full Fathom Five* and *Miss Nike Ajax*. His website is www.willhopkins4.com.

R.G. KOEPF has always been a writer, receiving her first rejection letter from *Jack and Jill Magazine* when she was ten years old. As a naval officer, she served as a Staff Writer in the White House Liaison Office for the Secretary of the Navy. An early resident of East Beach, she helped establish several neighborhood traditions, including Bible Study and the 4th of July Parade, and is a founding member of the East Beach Writers Guild. She now lives on Lake Gaston, North Carolina.

MARY-JAC O'DANIEL is originally from Richardson, Texas. She has a Bachelor of Science in Education from Baylor University and she is currently pursuing a Master's Degree in Speech Pathology from Old Dominion University. Mary-Jac is a former high school English teacher and track coach, who has taught in California and in China. An avid traveler, Mary-Jac has been able to visit every continent except Africa and Antarctica. She enjoys running, swimming, competitive sailing, and any excuse to have a glass of wine. Mary-Jac is a military spouse and lives in East Beach with her husband, Paul.

JAYNE ORMEROD grew up in a small Ohio town then went on to a small-town Ohio college. Upon earning her degree in accounting she became a CIA (that's not a sexy spy thing, but a Certified Internal Auditor.) She married a naval officer and off they sailed to see the world. After fifteen moves she realized she needed a more transportable vocation, so turned to writing cozy mysteries. To learn more about Jayne and her writings, please visit her website: www.JayneOrmerod.com.

MIKE OWENS, a retired physician, has undergraduate and medical degrees from the University of North Carolina in Chapel Hill. He obtained his MFA degree in creative writing from Old Dominion University in Norfolk, VA in 2011. His nonfiction works include: *Care of the Terminally Ill Cancer Patient* (2002) and *Primary Care Issues for End-of-Life Care* (2003). His first novel, *The End of Free Will*, was published in January, 2014, followed by a second novel, *The Threshold*, in September 2014. Website: www.MikeOwens42.com.

JENNY F. SPARKS was born and raised in South Carolina. She graduated from the College of Charleston with a BS in Sociology and a minor in Health and Gerontology. Married for 26 years to a career naval officer, she has lived throughout the United States and raised two sons. She has volunteered in various positions in her children's schools and with the Navy in jobs ranging from PTA president to ombudsman. She has been employed as a preschool teacher, vocational education teacher, vocational consultant and senior center director. Jenny lives in Virginia with her husband and their dogs, Millie and Twyla.

FOR MORE INFORMATION ABOUT THE AUTHORS

There's more to our stories! We've posted interviews and photos of our authors having fun on our blog: www.ByTheBayStories.blogspot.com.

And be sure join the discussion on our By the Bay Facebook page. On Wednesdays, the authors answer whimsical questions offered up by friends and fans.

Made in the USA
Charleston, SC
23 October 2015